PRAISE FOR *WE ARE TOTALLY NORMAL*:

"Told through the eyes of one of the most endearing and real characters I've ever met, *We Are Totally Normal* is validating, entertaining, and filled with love."
—**KACEN CALLENDER**, Stonewall Award–winning author of *This Is Kind of an Epic Love Story*

"A perfect story about the complications of sexuality and identity. I adored this book from beginning to end."
—**MASON DEAVER**, author of *I Wish You All the Best*

"An engrossing and palpable story that is in no rush to have all the answers, and that's totally normal."
—**SARA FARIZAN**, award-winning author of *Tell Me Again How a Crush Should Feel*

"Nandan's fresh perspective is a gift— I can't wait for readers to experience it!"
—**M-E GIRARD**, Lambda Literary Award–winning author of *Girl Mans Up*

"An endearing, messy, and honest exploration of identity that reminds us that discovering who we aren't is as important as discovering who we are."
—**SHAUN DAVID HUTCHINSON**, author of *We Are the Ants* and *Brave Face*

"A brilliant coming-of-age story. Every teen needs this book."
—**JULIAN WINTERS**, award-winning author of *Running with Lions*
and *How To Be Remy Cameron*

"Incisive, funny, and gloriously messy."
—**KELLY LOY GILBERT**, author of *Picture Us in the Light*

"A fresh and rare exploration of sexuality, identity, friendship,
and love."
—**DAHLIA ADLER**, author of *Under the Lights*

"Raw, intimate, and unflinchingly honest,
We Are Totally Normal fully embraces the messiness
and unpredictability of the human heart."
—**LAURIE ELIZABETH FLYNN**, author of *Firsts,*
Last Girl Lied To, and *All Eyes on Her*

WE ARE TOTALLY NORMAL

RAHUL KANAKIA

An Imprint of HarperCollinsPublishers

HarperTeen is an imprint of HarperCollins Publishers.

ISBN 978-0-06-286581-6

Typography by Corina Lupp
20 21 22 23 24 PC/LSCH 10 9 8 7 6 5 4 3 2 1

First Edition

WE ARE TOTALLY NORMAL

1

THE MUSIC IN THE CAR was so loud that my teeth vibrated. I couldn't hear words, just a raw, brutal wall of noise. I didn't cover my ears, since you shouldn't ever show that kind of weakness around Pothan and Ken, but half an hour into the ride I leaned forward and shouted: "Are we going to the lake house?"

"What?" Pothan yelled.

I reached for the volume knob, but Ken swatted my hand.

"Are we going to the lake house?" I shouted.

"What?"

"Are we going to the lake house?"

"What?"

This went on absurdly long, until I realized Pothan was toying with me. I slapped the back of his head, and he jerked the car into the next lane.

"Holy shit!" I yelped.

"Don't mess with the driver."

"You did that on purpose."

Ken sat quietly in the front passenger seat, his face lit up with a sideways smile. Ken had really dense eyebrows and a broad neck. His arms and shoulders were huge, but his legs were puny, and Pothan loved to call him chicken legs. Ken always said legs didn't matter; girls didn't go for legs, but I was sure he regretted his gym choices—he never, under any circumstances, wore shorts. The problem was that if he suddenly added a leg day to his workout, everyone would know Pothan had gotten to him.

When they missed the exit for the lake house, I was like, *What the fuck?*, but Pothan pretended not to notice.

"Hey, where are we going?"

"You'll see."

"Umm, didn't Avani say to meet at the lake house?"

"Nandan, this is an intervention. You cannot keep trying to hang out with her."

Part of me wanted to force Ken and Pothan to let me out and let me make my own way to the lake house. But if I showed up by myself, empty-handed, without a party in tow, it wouldn't be fun: it'd be stilted and awkward.

I wasn't like Pothan. I didn't have that indefinable extra something that marked a person as a leader. A party isn't an end in itself; a party is just a container for exciting things. It's a place

2

where you bring together lots of people and heat them up and see what will happen. But in order to experience the magic and grandeur of a party, you need to hang around the right people. My presence brought nothing extra to a party, and I'd resigned myself to this. I was a follower.

We ended up at the beach, in Santa Cruz, where Pothan and Ken made me gulp down a forty before letting me out of the car. I was ambling across the boardwalk, grinning goofily, when Pothan jabbed my side and said to look for a rebound girl.

I rubbed the sore spot on my rib and looked for an opening to hit him back, but he was already out of arm's reach.

"Avani made you lazy," Pothan said. "She was a decent start, but you got lucky, bro. Admit it, you got lucky."

"I freely admit she was out of my league," I said.

"Nobody's out of your league, dude. That attitude is exactly the problem. You act like you're not good enough, and the problem is that doesn't work. If you're not confident, most girls can smell that, and they stay away."

We ate hot dogs at a table on the edge of the boardwalk. To our left, tourists spilled out of a Ripley's, and on our right, the ocean was lit by the setting sun.

A dozen feet away, a group of three girls burst into laughter. I fought to catch the nearest girl's eye, and she smiled back with that nervous, automatic smile that's a girl's first defense against a strange guy.

"Should we talk to them?" I said.

"Who?" Pothan said. "Them?" He jabbed a thumb at the trio, and over his shoulder I saw them notice his gesture. "No. Of course not."

Ken looked up from his phone. "The blind spot should be pretty good today." They were talking about the part of the beach, out past the rocks, that you couldn't see from the boardwalk.

"Yep. The blind spot," Pothan said.

I compacted all my food trash into a ketchup-covered ball and tossed it into the garbage can. The eyes of the girls tracked us. Ken tossed a brutal "Hey" in their direction, but we were gone before they could respond.

"Uhh, maybe I don't understand the plan here," I said.

"Dude," Ken said. "You're gonna hook up *today*. Those girls? They would've laughed and smiled and maybe followed you online, but here and now nothing would've happened."

Pothan clapped a hand onto Ken's shoulder. "Hey, there's nothing wrong with planting seeds for later."

My neck was tense. I was actually fine with later. Somewhere out of sight. Hooking up in the blind spot, with the whole beach nearby, sounded incredibly nerve-racking.

We climbed over the rocks and came down near a group of kids sitting on the other side. They wore dark colors, and many had dyed hair. Leather jackets were in evidence. You know, it's weird: you watch old movies and the alternative kids are always wearing the exact same shit that alternative kids wear today.

They gave us blank, guarded looks, but Pothan jabbed his

chin at them, and although my stomach squawked, I knew this was a test of whether I had the balls to approach.

"Err, hey."

I spoke to the group in general, but my voice was quiet and the surf was loud, and only one guy, a dude with three earrings through his left ear, looked at me.

"Hey," I said again.

"Yeah?"

"Umm, what's up?"

"Nothing, 'bruh,'" he said. "What's up with you?"

One of the girls looked me over and turned away. Then Pothan came in, with his back hunched, his arms hanging down like a crazed monkey. "Yo," he said. "You guys have any rolling papers?"

The guy shrugged. Then there was a general rooting-through of bags until a pack of rolling papers appeared. Taking the little cardboard package, Pothan said, "Cool. Oh, anyone have something I can use for a filter?"

Ken, to my side, started snickering.

A longer wait while a girl tore off a little bit of the cover from her notebook. "Great, great," Pothan said. "Now anyone got any tobacco?"

A pouch was produced. By now half the group had figured out the joke, but their leader, the guy with the earrings, was still huffing and puffing and shaking his head, as if to be like, *Okay, fine, now it's time for you to leave.*

I jumped in. "Let me do that." I took over the spliff-rolling operation while Pothan made small talk with the leader.

"Umm," I said. "Anyone got any weed I can put in here?"

There was open laughter. The nearest girl, thank God, took out a little grinder and sprinkled some onto the paper. I gave her a big smile. Her hair was pink, but it'd grown out, showing her dark roots. I scooted close, sitting cross-legged with the paper on my lap.

"Hey," I said. My heart was beating so hard, and for once not just from anxiety, but from excitement too. "Help shield me from the wind."

She put out her hands. "You guys are ridiculous," she said.

"Believe me, I know."

I blinked a few times and looked at the little mass of weed and tobacco lying on the paper.

"Anyone have . . . ?" I said.

The whole group stopped talking.

"The knowledge of how to, umm, actually roll this?"

More laughter. By now Ken and Pothan were sitting too. I looked with innocent eyes at the girl, and she shook her head and took everything off my hands. After that, we talked a bit more naturally. I lay down with my head in the girl's lap, and she fell to stroking my hair. The joint passed, but I didn't intercept it. The conversation swirled above me while her fingers went through my hair again and again.

"You're so tangled," she said.

"These two assholes grabbed me out of bed before I could shower."

A hairbrush appeared, and she worked it gently through my hair, tugging here and there at knots. Her other hand massaged my ear, scraping out a little of the sand that'd collected inside. Everything was so incredibly perfect. The girl and I smiled at each other. I didn't know her name, and I didn't want to know it.

Ken's laughter broke through. "What the fuck is going on there?"

I got up, shaking my hair, and the girl pulled away, embarrassed, even though we hadn't *done* anything.

"Nothing," I said. "Just brushing out the sand."

She put the brush back in her bag, and shortly after, her group was like, *We gotta run.* Ken gave them an awkward-as-hell invite to party with us, but Pothan waved goodbye and made for the next group of people.

I chased after the alternative kids for a few feet, until I was walking backward in front of the girl. "Hey. Thanks," I said.

Her expression was so strange. Mouth completely flat; eyes downcast. But after I spoke, her lips turned upward in a tiny smile. The whole group was tense, and I understood their feelings, but I hated being treated like a possible predator.

"No problem," she said.

After a half beat, I tossed her another helpless smile and ran back to Pothan.

Ken gave me shit for not making a move, but Pothan shook his head. "Your only problem was you gave her all the power. Like, from the ground, you couldn't do shit, she had all the control, and that made her feel safe, but you were also powerless, and that meant she wasn't into you."

"Whatever, I liked it."

He grabbed me around the middle while Ken glowered at us. "That's cool, bro. You've gotta have some fun. Not every girl is closable."

"I could've done it," Ken said.

"Dude, don't be like that," Pothan said. "He's just *learning*. He's not a Jedi master like you and me."

We launched into another group of kids, and this one was a disaster. A beefy guy threatened to kick our asses, and we ran away, jumping up and screeching like a pod of dolphins. The next group was all college girls, a row of shining bodies—one was on her stomach, bikini top unhooked so she wouldn't have tan lines—and we were a troop of clowns, performing for them, pretending we were visiting scientists from MIT, here for a conference, and they laughed and laughed until the laughter trailed off, and after a few minutes it got weird, so I checked out, saying I needed to pee.

The silvery seas let loose a distant howl, and with every step my smile got wider. The nearest bathroom had no line, but I texted the guys that I was headed to the far one that nobody uses.

After I'd pissed, I looked across the sand, thought about Pothan and Ken still swirling around those girls, and decided I could take a few more minutes, so I stood in line for a churro. Imagining how Ken would probably lick and suck on the churro and make some gross remarks, continuing the joke until the humor dried up and the laughter turned uncomfortable, made me glad I was alone.

Then a bright purple bow tie walked past my table.

"Dave!" I said. "Hey, Dave."

The wind was loud, and he walked past unhearing, so I ran half a step and said, "Dave, dude. What's up?"

Bow Tie Dave was my project. I always saw him hanging around the edges of parties, getting way too drunk, not really saying much, but the thing is—he was actually kind of hot. Maybe folks didn't see it because he was Asian, and they were used to looking past him, but he had an interesting body—thin hipped and broad shouldered—that gave him a hawklike look. His face was nice too, with its high cheekbones and straight nose. In his glasses and blazer he was an Asian Clark Kent. And everybody knows it's not the fifties anymore: nowadays girls think Clark Kent is way hotter than Superman.

"Hey, dude," I said. "What you doing here?"

"Oh . . . I actually work at the Baskin-Robbins."

"Nice. I didn't know that."

"Yep, I job. I'm a job haver. Ever since I was fourteen."

"Is that even legal?"

"At ice-cream stores? I don't know. I think ice-cream stores exist in a weird legal limbo. As long as your fingers are strong enough to grip the scoopers, you're good."

I laughed. "Hey, uhh, what happened with that girl you asked me about?"

"Mari?" He shook his head. "Disaster. I'm awful. I'm the worst. We hung out for *six hours* yesterday on the boardwalk."

"That doesn't seem bad."

"I couldn't even hold her hand," he said.

"Shit."

"Yeah, that's it. You're making the right face to describe this situation."

I tried to smile. "Come on, dude, you want a churro? Let's get a churro."

"You just ate a churro."

"Let's get *another* churro. What? A guy can't eat multiple churros in one day? You don't know my life. You don't know my struggle. Stop food-shaming me."

He looked over his shoulder, as if expecting rescue, but I grabbed the sleeve of his collared shirt and gave it a slight tug. As we were ordering the churros, my phone buzzed.

Pothan: Dude, where are you?

Me: Can't talk. Met a friend. Be right back.

I pocketed my phone. Dave said, "Are the guys waiting for you?"

"Don't worry," I said. "We've got time."

The picnic tables were filled, so we leaned against the wooden railing. The wind beat against the collar of Dave's shirt, and my eyes were drawn to a little smudge of sugar at the corner of his mouth.

"It was a disaster," he said. "Like, after dropping her off, I just sat in my car and laughed. She must be like, *What just happened?* And I even *called* it a date. I was like, 'Let's go out on a date.' But then I made zero moves."

"No, no." I nodded my head. "I get it."

"But do you actually? Or are you just trying to relate? Because shyness doesn't seem like a problem you have."

"Mmm."

"I've *seen* you."

"Things happen."

"I kinda never want to see her again."

"Dude, I get it. Do you know why Avani and I stopped hooking up?"

His eyebrows went up.

"Too much stress!" I said. "Every time we were together, I'd be like, *Will we hook up? Where's this going? What's happening? Will she talk to me? Will she ignore me?* I hated it. Half the time I was so anxious I couldn't even get it up." Although that was my deepest and most shameful secret, it slipped out easily with

11

Dave. "Then one day I was like, *Wait a second, if I end things first, I'll win.* So I did."

"But . . . she really liked you."

"No. That's not true. I don't know."

A jet plane left a long white mark on the sky. "It wasn't fun. None of this is any fun."

He doubled over, dropping his head into his hand. "It's like a math problem. How do we make it fun?"

"I have no idea. You only get these tiny, brief, infinitesimal moments of fun. And then, no fun. The fun disappears."

"We don't *have* to do this. We could just ignore it all."

"Yeah. . . ."

Dave looked up at me. "You're not convinced."

"I don't know, dude. Those moments, though . . ."

His eyebrows crinkled. "What? What're you thinking about?"

"Dave, you're supposed to just let people trail off into silence."

He rolled his eyes. "Come on. Talking to you is like the only excitement I ever get in my life."

"Well, I don't know, I had this weird moment. . . ." I told him about the girl running the brush through my hair on the beach. As the words came out, I saw details I hadn't noticed at the time, like the way her eyes, seen from below, were so watery and insubstantial.

"And you didn't even ask her name?"

"No. I didn't want it."

"Maybe you're turning into one of those awkward-cool guys."

"What?"

"You know what I'm talking about?" he said. "Those guys everybody loves. Like, umm, umm, Greg Sarbanes."

"I don't know who that is."

"Or Hyram Willendowski."

"Who?"

"Niko Diamandis?"

"The kid who wears a fanny pack?"

"He never makes *any* moves, but all the girls love him. It's kind of amazing to watch. This is our idol, Nandan."

"Whose idol? Not my idol."

"He's an idol for nerdy guys. Like, you guys—nonawkward guys—have Pothan. We have Niko. He's completely oblivious to everything and everyone. And he talks alllllll the time about how terrible he is with girls, and you can see them just looking at him and being like, *But you're so hot, you're so amazing, except maybe you don't know you're hot. Maybe you need my help, my sexual help, to get over your awkwardness.*"

"But he wears a fanny pack."

"I'm telling you, dude."

Now I laughed. "Okay, so go to Niko for advice."

"You think I haven't tried?" he said. "The thing is . . . ninety-nine percent of cool people—basically all of them, aside from you—are incapable of being honest."

"About what?"

"I don't know!"

"You're not making sense, dude."

He rubbed his fingers together. "I mean I'm not Holden Caulfield. I think being a fake is great. I wish I was a fake. But you have to let people behind the mask sometimes. Niko never does. If I was like, 'How do I get with Mari?' he'd be like, 'Why are you asking me? I'm so terrible with girls. I'm suuuuuch a geek.'"

The way he said that, all nasal and drawn-out, made me laugh, and I ruffled the swoop of his hair.

"Hey!"

"No, but I believe you," I said. "About Niko. The thing is, there are people like him, who've got the magic, and people like us, who need to fake it."

"You don't fake it."

"I'm in so over my head. Pothan's trying to turn me into"—I thought of trying to hook up with some random girl, maybe tonight, maybe over by the rocks, and my stomach lurched—"into a completely different person. But the crazy thing is: I *want* to be that person."

Dave brushed sugar crumbs off his fingers. "Well, to be honest, I'd prefer not to change completely just to get a girl-friend."

"I don't know, though," I said. "There's so much shit that nobody teaches you. I'm talking about all that garbage that Pothan and Ken believe in, stuff like how you've gotta sack up

14

and be a warrior and never show fear. That's all true. It's all really true. Because without that you're just nobody."

Dave tipped up his glasses, rubbing the bridge of his nose, and the air whipped his fine hair off to the side.

"I've just got to make a move on Mari," he said. "I've got to make a move."

I nodded. "Pretty much."

My phone buzzed again.

Pothan: What the hell, where are you?

The sun kissed the ocean, and all the heat seemed to sizzle out of the sand. I pulled my hoodie closer and said, "Hey, you want to come hang out?"

"I've gotta go back to work."

"What about after? You could invite Mari! Give it another shot, seriously, dude."

He looked down; then his eyes went back to me. "Sure. I can give it a try."

"Do it!" I said. "We're gonna make this happen."

I got up, nodding my head, and left with a big smile.

While I was gone, Pothan and Ken had regrouped at the car. They handed me another forty, and after I'd gotten a third of the way through, they told me to lean back against the door, and Pothan put out his hands.

"Now don't freak out," he said.

"All right. . . ."

"But we invited Avani to come down."

"Dude," I said. "She's not gonna come. She's done with the beach scene. That's why she asked us to the lake house."

"She's on her way, dude." Pothan held up his phone. "I just got the text."

My heart quivered. "Oh."

I must've looked anxious, because Pothan grabbed my neck. "Whatever, dude, just be cool."

"No, it's really not a problem."

"And no hanging around her. Stick with us. You've gotta be cool."

Pothan shook his head, and now he used a finger to tip the bottle in my hand, trying to get me to drink up. A rush of foam surged onto my face, and the bottle fell to the pavement and shattered in a spray of beer and glass.

2

AVANI WAS STILL A HALF hour away, so we hung out in Ken's car. Nobody talked about their feelings or anything at all real, but it wasn't unfun. At one point the cops buzzed past, and we hit the floor, and fifteen minutes later we were still crouched in the back and in the wheel wells, passing the two remaining bottles between us, laughing and pressing up against each other. Pothan got on top of Ken, humping him, and Ken rolled his eyes back, pretending to enjoy it.

Ken made fun of me for being weird around Avani.

"Dude," I said. "I'm happy she and I are broken up."

"Except you were never together."

"Then why did we have a breakup conversation?"

"That was all you. Nobody thought you needed to do that."

"I just wanted to stay friends."

"LOL, you regret it, dude," Ken said. "No shame in that. Just admit you regret it."

"But I don't."

"Whatever."

"Hey, hey," Pothan said. "He didn't want her to get attached. That's fine, dude. You should've done the same thing with Laila."

Even in the dim light, I saw Ken's ears turn red. This sophomore girl Laila had stopped responding to Ken's texts, and Pothan kept harping on it. Pothan was like a wolf—he'd find your weak point and attack it, again and again, until you showed your belly.

"Dude," I said. "Lay off about that."

"Look," Ken said, "Laila was *crazy*."

"Crazy for your dick, until you effed it up."

My phone flashed. Dave had texted: his shift was ending. I wrote that I was in the car with Pothan and Ken, watching them try to psychologically dominate each other. It'd be fascinating to create a video game that modeled how guys spend their time testing out weak points, pushing and pulling and slapping and wrestling, to see who's in charge and who isn't. Normally Pothan was on top, but Ken had been trying him lately. I was a year younger and usually wasn't part of the contest, but my trying to get Pothan to stop making fun of Ken had put Ken in competition with *me*—when you protect someone, you're sort of saying you're better than them—so he started in on Avani again.

"You were scared," Ken said. "You were like a dude who's harpooned a whale. You want to reel her in, but you can't."

I said, "The whale's your mom, right?"

Pothan whooped, and I popped the door, saying I needed to piss.

I staggered off into the dunes, with Pothan and Ken running and shouting behind me. I found a cactus and pissed facing them, because they'd been known to try to hit me with their spray.

Avani's immense gray SUV bounced over the curb and lurched into the parking lot. The car stopped at the far corner, and an unearthly blue lit up the interior. All three girls in the car were hunched over their phones.

Fierce winds blew off the sea, and as families streamed away from the boardwalk, I saw, here and there, groups of kids moving purposefully toward the beach. When night fell, the real fun started.

I wiped my hands on my jeans, and I watched Avani's car, thinking about those three girls—she always came with her friends Carrie and Jessie—sitting in its cool black interior, and my heart lurched. Maybe Pothan was right. Maybe I was hung up on Avani, but the thought of her didn't make me angry or ashamed or sad. Instead, whenever she showed up, I became purely, immensely happy.

My phone lit with a text.

Avani: We're here. Where are you guys?

Abandoning Ken and Pothan, I walked toward her car.

The door slid open, and Jessie shouted, "Nandan! Thank God!"

Avani's voice: "I *told* you he was here."

Jessie gave me an awkward one-armed hug. The moment I was in, I pulled the door closed, sealing myself inside. Jessie's dirty-blond hair was pulled back in a ponytail, and she was in a puffy vest and hiking boots and jeans. I flashed her a smile.

"Hey," I said. "What's up?"

"So are the guys really here?"

"Yeah, sorry about the lake house, by the way."

I instantly knew that mentioning it had been a mistake. I'd suggested a dozen times that Avani invite us to the lake house, and now she'd done it and we hadn't come. Avani ignored my apology.

"Where are they?" she said.

Avani was a shadowy figure in the driver's seat. Her keys hung around her wrist, attached to a bracelet, and her eyes, despite the setting sun, were veiled by sunglasses.

"Uhh, they're peeing in the dunes."

"Why?" Carrie said. "Aren't there bathrooms?"

I paused for a second. "Actually there are. That's a really good question."

20

"That's gross," Jessie said. "Why do those guys do that? Pee on the dunes for no reason? Isn't that bad for the environment?"

"Yessssss," I said. "These are great questions."

"Please," Avani said. "Nandan's probably peed out there a hundred times. He's no different from the rest. You are way too easy on him, Jess."

"Whoa, whoa, whoa," I said. "Too mean."

Ever since we had stopped hooking up, Avani had taken to lashing out in this same way, always implying I was just as shallow and immature as all the other guys.

I didn't get it, but I also didn't hate it. All my life people had been like, *Oh, Nandan, you're different. You're deeper. You're more sensitive.* Now at least one person was saying the opposite, and it felt nice. Maybe that showed just how much I had changed in the past year.

Carrie turned around in her seat. "What's up, dude?"

She was a tiny brown-skinned Vietnamese girl with bobbed hair and a fierce attitude. Right now she wore slacks and black boots and a wool halter-top deal underneath a huge windbreaker.

Avani, on the other hand, had long, wild black hair and seemed to have dressed according to a completely different color scheme: she was in white pants, a yellow T-shirt, and a tan leather jacket—all accentuated by the many-colored bracelets on her right wrist.

21

Avani hopped out and opened the trunk. As I joined her around back, she said: "What's going on? What are we doing?"

"Here's the thing." I put two hands together as if I were praying. "I don't know that there's a very well-formulated plan."

"God."

One school really shouldn't hold both an Avani and a Pothan. It creates conflict. She was grabbing blankets and chairs—all the little stuff that guys forget—and meanwhile Pothan rolled up and, assessing the situation in a split second, leaned on Jessie, asking her what was going on, distracting her from Avani's orders. They fought a tug-of-war—Avani gave commands; Pothan ignored or laughed at them—and I came up next to Avani, giving her a conspiratorial smile.

"Hey," I said. "Let me take something."

"Great."

She dropped a duffel bag into my arms and told me to find a spot on the beach and turned without checking to see if I'd heard. She gave a nod to Carrie, and some silent communication passed between them. Carrie walked off a little ways and made a call. I imagined the two of them as CIA agents, supervising the cleanup from some covert operation, and a weak smile hit my lips.

Avani had enveloped me in silence. So long as I held her duffel, I wasn't a part of this group—in their minds I was already gone—and none of the girls paid any attention to me.

Pothan told me to drop that shit and come with him to buy more beer.

"No, I'll, uhh, I'll do this."

"Seriously, dude. What is wrong with you? It's over."

I carried the duffel bag to the other side of the rocks, where the waves, now in low tide, had left behind hundreds of yards of mucky-soft sands. I opened the duffel, got out the blankets, and laid them on a dry patch of sand, next to a firepit. In the distance, about a hundred yards away, another group of kids was clustered around a bonfire. Up on the cliffs, silent cars pulsed through the curves of Highway 1.

I texted Avani, saying I'd found a good spot. Then I saw a message from Dave.

Dave: Mari is on her way. Wish me luck!
Me: You two are staying here? Come by the blind spot! I think there's gonna be a to-do? A foofaraw? Not sure of the technical terminology.
Dave: You might be thinking of the term "hoedown."
Me: Pretty sure you need bales of straw for that.

My fingers flew across the phone, sending energy through the ether, directly into Dave's brain. Texting him was different from texting Avani. He responded instantly. Like he actually wanted and needed me around. I just wished that I didn't feel so . . . so . . . so . . . sick for her presence. I didn't want to hook up with her—that was done, I knew—but even those few seconds in the car with her and Carrie and Jessie, earlier, had felt *so* right.

What Pothan forgot was that Avani and I had always been friends! We'd hung out for months before we started "hanging out." And we talked about stuff too! I told her all my crazy theories about how to get ahead. Heard about her constant friendship drama with Carrie. We'd spend hours sitting in silence in her basement, drinking from the cup of each other's company. And when we weren't together, we were texting. Just gossip. Or little jokes. But it'd been so important—that sense of being always connected to another person. And now it was ruined.

Dave was totally game to come out, and in ten minutes I saw a tall form striding toward me. He was with a girl, short and a little chubby, whose smile I saw from thirty feet away.

The figure waved an arm, and I waved back.

We met in a nowhere spot, a few blankets set down at the edge of a little cove of rocks, and most of the light came from the intersecting beams of our phones.

"This is cool," the girl said. "So this is where it happens? The rich beautiful people getting into trouble on the beach stuff?"

"Hey, I'm Nandan."

"Mari!" she said. "Dave! You're supposed to introduce me!"

The three of us sat down, folding the edges of the blankets over our laps to provide some shelter. The song of the wind got louder, and now it blew sand off the rocks and into our faces.

Avani: Thanks for finding a spot! Can you get some driftwood? Pothan is being a dick, but I'll get him out there soon.
Me: Sure.

Mari peered over my shoulder. "What is it? What's happening?"

"Avani wants me to gather driftwood," I said.

"I can help!" Mari said.

The blanket was held tight around her shoulders, and she looked heavy and padded and crone-like.

"What?" I said. "No. No. . . . No. We are not doing this."

"Huh?"

"Come on, let's pick up all this stuff," I said. "Wait, actually let's just leave it here."

Crossing to the other side of the rocks instantly halved the wind. We walked far from the dying lights of the boardwalk. I had texted Avani that I'd left the blankets behind, and now I was afraid to look at my phone.

Mari chattered between us, and Dave hardly said a word. He pulled away from Mari when she reached for his hand to get help climbing over the rocks.

Pulling myself out of my own head, I said, "Uhh, did you drive here?"

"My mom dropped me off!" Mari said.

"Seriously? Your mom dropped you off at the Santa Cruz boardwalk after dark?"

"Why?" she said. "Is that stupid? My mom would *love* to hear this. She's always wondering if she's a bad mom." Her fingers flew over her phone. "Just told my mom the consensus is that she did something stupid. Okay, now she's texting back. 'WHYYYYYYYYYYY?'"

"I don't know. . . ." I shrugged. I didn't want to imply she was too close to her mom. That was the sort of thing that Pothan and Avani did. They put people down, just to make themselves look better. It was like making people wait for you. It was automatic. Something that reinforced the idea you were better than them.

"What?" she said. "What were you gonna say?"

"Uhh, it's no big deal. Most people come here to escape their parents, but you and your mom are cool with each other, and that's awesome."

"I didn't know there was anything to worry about!" Mari said. "She loves Dave!"

As we came to the end of the rocks, I saw a big bunch of kids standing at one end, near the century-old wooden roller coaster. I waved a hand, and we slowly approached.

Avani looked at me with confusion. "Oh, hey . . . ," she said.

Carrie was there, too, but things had gotten weird between her and Avani. She was talking to this other girl I didn't recognize. Pothan tugged a beer out of his jacket pocket and lobbed it in my direction. My catch went wrong, and I slapped the can into the sand, stinging my fingers.

"What's up?" Pothan said.

I introduced my friends. Mari, so talkative a second ago, went completely silent, while Dave answered only with shrugs and "Hmms" when Pothan asked him stuff.

We merged with the group, and I got hugs and fist bumps from the people I knew. Jessie acted really happy to see me, and she apologized, in a whisper, for abandoning me. "Carrie's girlfriend showed up with some other Holy Redeemer girls."

"Ohhh . . ." I glanced quickly at the girl, who, wearing jeans and a hoodie instead of the Redeemer uniform, seemed the same as a Grenadine High girl.

Avani ignored me; she caught up in the orbit of Henry, the only openly gay guy among our group of friends. I insinuated myself into their circle and waited for my chance to join the bantering.

Maybe it's a stereotype, but some people are just really gay. They have soft wavy hair, they buy clothes that fit really well, and they say everything with a sardonic, half-joking tone. Henry told me once that when he realized he was gay, it was frustrating, because he was like, *Ughhhhh, my parents were right!*

Apparently they'd been hinting to him that he might be queer since like age six.

"Nandan!" Hen said. "You are my hero. You are my idol. You are . . ."

"What . . . ?" I said. "What's happening?"

"Your pants. They're incredible."

They were garishly embroidered bell-bottom jeans, bought from a thrift store. "Thanks."

For the first time Avani looked at me. "Nandan has no eye," she said.

"What the . . . ?" I shook my head. "I think Henry is saying the opposite."

"Oh . . . relax." She wrapped an arm around me, and we both let the warm glow of Henry's voice fall over us. We were in the darkness cast by the roller coaster, and all the faces were indistinct. Avani rested her head against my shoulder.

"You two were so perfect together," Henry said.

The polarity had switched. Henry's attention dragged Carrie and her girlfriend toward us. Dave and Mari were still hovering nearby, and I introduced them to Avani, and she exerted herself to actually be *nice* to them. We laughed and had fun. I even teased Avani about the blankets I'd left beyond the rocks.

She got mad, saying I could've at least brought them back. She stomped off, trying to find somebody to help her get them. I was about to follow, but Henry shook his head.

"Don't humor her," he said.

He was right. When I took a few steps in her direction, she was arrogant and cold again.

"I'm not gonna fuck you just because you helped me carry some blankets," she said.

"Whoa," I said. "What the hell? Come on, Avani. That's not what I want."

Avani's response to my trying to be friends was to pretend *she* had ended things with *me*. "Sure, whatever."

I put up my hands and circled back to Henry, who was trying to pull Mari into a conversation. Hen had a fluid grace and languid voice that made everything seem *so* simple. I got drunker and drunker, laughing and shouting with the rest. Avani came back and slapped me in the face for some reason. Dave and Mari stayed in the background, no matter how many times I tried to draw them out, but I kept an eye on the two of them even as they hovered around the edges of the crowd.

Then, between one moment and the next, Mari disappeared.

3

MY FOGGY BRAIN WAS SLOW to grasp that Mari was gone.

"But where is she?" I said.

"Her mom got her," Dave said.

At our backs, I heard shouting and a brief flash of light. Then more pops. Roman candles had sprouted from everybody's hands, and my friends ran around shooting them at each other like guns. Pothan shot a full round of flares at Avani, and I put a hand to my mouth, wondering if her hair would catch fire, but they all glanced off her sweatshirt.

Carrie ran toward us, her mouth wide open. "Here," she said. "Here! I got them online." Her backpack was full of the flame sticks. She jangled the bag at us. I took one, and fire snapped from a metal lighter in her hand. The end of my Roman candle was alight.

"Shit!" I pointed it at Pothan, but Dave tipped my hand, and I shot the flares into the sand.

"Dude," he said. "You could hurt someone."

I shook my head. "Uhh, huh?" In a few seconds the firework was spent, and Carrie's backpack was empty, and everybody stood still, shrieking and laughing.

"That was so epic." Pothan grabbed Carrie and lifted her up. "Carrie, you are a monster!"

Now more beers were popped. Avani sat on a concrete divider, staring blankly at the ground. I knew she hated how people like Carrie and Pothan needed to disrupt perfectly good parties with their crazy, attention-getting stunts. Normally, at this point I'd go to her and she'd cry, and, with alcohol and loneliness to blunt her normal resentment, we might manage for a few hours to be friends again. But today I had Dave by my side, still looking a little shell-shocked.

"Why'd Mari leave?"

Dave shook his head. "Hey, dude," he said. "I think I'm gonna go. Do you need a ride?"

"What?"

"Umm . . . are you okay?"

"I'm fine."

My brain wasn't working. I held on to his forearm and blinked a few times. Then I drunkenly teleported into his car. Dave's face was lit up by the brightness of his phone.

"What's happening?" I said. "It's only . . ." I looked at my phone. "It's only ten o'clock."

"I'm gonna head out," he said. "I have a class tomorrow."

"But it's summer. . . ."

"It's an SAT class."

"Right . . . coo . . ."

"But you should get back. You're right, it's only ten."

"No, uhh, du-dude. Dude." My finger at this point might've been jabbing him in the chest. "We need to debrief. You know—post—postgame analysis of, uhh, she was cute. I liked her! So cute!"

"Mmm-hmmm. I don't know. She and I are probably not gonna happen."

"Why not?! She liked you."

"I couldn't make the move."

He started the car. And in the dim light from the dashboard panels, his face stood out cold and serious, with a little shock of hair askew over his forehead. He was small and dejected and dirty, and even his bow tie was crooked.

"Last chance to get out and go back to the party," he said.

"No, no way. You're my bro, and a bro has to bro with his bros."

"Okay, fine."

Then we were on Highway 1, and I watched the dark ocean tumble against the cliffs below.

✴ ✴ ✴

We lived in Grenadine, on the other side of the hills, and the drive was a long one. I looked at my phone, expecting a text from one of my friends asking where I'd gone, and when it didn't come I gathered a bouquet of sadness and bitterness and clutched it to my chest.

Then I remembered Hen, reaching out to me through the darkness and silence. I admired him. He had burst onto the scene during our freshperson year—we'd gone to the same middle school, but before coming out he'd been nobody. Maybe it isn't politically correct to say, but being gay was pretty cool—it was a specialness, a separateness, that couldn't be challenged.

Carrie was the same. Though for her it'd been harder. When she'd told people she was bisexual, they'd thought she only wanted attention, but ever since getting with Gabriela, the Holy Redeemer girl, she'd slowly formed her own unique reputation.

Sometimes I wondered if maybe I was a little bit gay. The idea of being with a dude didn't make me sick, like it seemed to make some guys. Sometimes I thought it'd be fun. Different. Easier.

Yet at the same time the idea of coming out felt shameful. It'd be so needy. So dishonest. I'd mentioned once to Pothan that I liked Hen's social role—his position at the intersection of every group—and Pothan had been like, "You drama queen, you'd just love being gay, wouldn't you?" And I'd flushed very red. Pothan had this way of seeing directly into my lightless core.

Right now the darkness of the passenger seat felt very safe. I fiddled around with the stations, changing all of Dave's presets.

"I'd tell you to stop, but I know you won't."

"No classical music. You're a young person, for Christ's sake."

"That's definitely a true statement," he said.

"Hey, dude, what happened with you and Mari? You two were doing so good."

"The thing is, I know, on some crazy abstract level, that it's possible for a person to be into me," he said. "And I have friends, right? So what do I want? Just a friend to have sex with. That seems pretty doable." Now he grimaced. "But then I look at myself in the mirror, and it seems impossible to believe anyone could ever like me."

"That's bullshit." My eyes swept across his face in profile: his dark hair brushed sideways across his forehead, his adorable glasses, and his strong neck disappearing into that collared shirt. "You're hot. You're smart. You're funny. Most guys are complete dicks. Girls would kill for somebody like you."

"Yeah, that's what people say. . . ." He shook his head. "I don't know. If I keep talking like this, I'll come off like a self-pitying monster. It's okay—nobody *owes* me anything."

"Dude, dude, dude, somewhere out there a girl is drawing hearts around your name." That was a line Pothan had used on me, earlier this summer, and I still wondered if it was actually true, but, whatever, it sounded good.

Then we were in front of my little apartment block, which was right off El Camino, across from a gas station and a Starbucks.

"Hey," I said. "What you up to now?"

Dave's pale nose and throat were lit up by the floodlights of the gas station. "Going home. Why? Is something happening?"

"We could keep hanging out."

He shrugged. "Sure."

"Yeah?"

I put a hand on the door and hopped into the cold air.

Each night before she leaves, my mom opens every single window, so when I got home the apartment was dim and drafty. But I turned on the heater and went around closing the windows.

"Just sit anywhere."

"Hey," Dave said, "do you have a towel?"

I saw his point: sand and salt were dried into my hairline and the folds of my eyes.

I blinked. "To sit on? Yeah."

But I didn't get the towels right away. Instead, I fiddled around with the stereo in the corner, tuning in to a Top 40 station. I bounced up and down on my heels as the music played, then stuck my head into the linen closet. Our apartment was tiny. After my dad died a few years ago, we'd had to leave our house, but my mom hadn't wanted to move to a cheaper town, because the school district was so good, so we'd gotten this place instead.

"You could just borrow some clothes," I said. "I'm not that much bigger."

"Maybe that's a good idea. I'm so gross. On the beach it doesn't matter, but the moment you get off the beach, it's like, why would anyone *ever* kiss me?"

The music still played dimly as we went into my room, and when he went through the door his eyebrows went up.

"This is kind of a collection."

The walls used to be covered in old movie posters I'd found in a stationery store: *Kill Bill*, *Scarface*, *The Godfather*. I'd watched some of them but wasn't really a movie guy. I just wanted to bring Avani back to something other than blank, bare walls. Then Avani had laughed at me for having such a guy's room, so I'd torn down half the movies and replaced them with girlier ones: *Mean Girls*, *High School Musical*, *When Harry Met Sally*. Now my room was exactly half and half.

"There's a story behind that," I said.

I jumped on the bed. By now my clothes had dried, and I didn't really care about the musty smell. He went through my closet.

"Most of the ones in that pile on the floor are clean too."

"Umm . . ."

He picked up a pair of khakis.

"No," I said. "Those are so torn."

"Err . . . ," he said. "Do you have any, like, normal clothes?"

"What?" I said.

Leaning over the side, I picked up a pair of jeans. "These are normal."

"They've got butterflies all over them."

"What're you, a homophobe? I feel very microaggressed right now."

His face froze, and Dave didn't relax until I smiled. I tossed him the jeans and some other clothes. "Hey, you can change in the bathroom."

While Dave was gone, my body odor wafted through the room and finally reached my nose, so my armpits got a once-over from some deodorant and I swapped out my clothes too, pulling on a red T-shirt—it showed two unicorns having sex—and a pair of dull brown pants.

Shower sounds had started in the bathroom, so I felt safe to fish out my secret supply of whiskey and mix it in the kitchen with some apple juice. The alcohol spread through my toes and fingers, and I became euphoric and relaxed and ready to gossip.

When he came out, I asked immediately, "So what did you think?"

"Huh?"

"Oh, haha, sorry. Here." I offered him some whiskey, and he shook his head. I took another gulp. I threw the living room's couch cushions on the floor and sat amid the pile. "Did you at least have fun? We're gonna do this again, you know that, right? Now you're, like, one of my peoples. I marked you as a peoples of mine."

"Uh . . ." He nodded slowly. "Maybe that ought to offend me, but . . ." He shrugged. "I'm a born follower. I've always known it."

"That makes two of us."

"What're you talking about? You're definitely not a follower."

"I am. And I don't care. I just wish I had a better leader."

"You are so drunk right now."

He laid his head against my side, and my hand reached up, sort of touched his chest. His other hand was uncomfortably close to my crotch, and I wriggled to one side.

"I don't know," I said. "I texted with Avani all week trying to get together a nice and chill day at the lake house. But Pothan ruined everything. They're in a fight, those two—a fight for the soul of the Ninety-Nine. All Pothan cares about is getting drunk on the beach. But Avani wants so much more, and I keep trying to help her, but she doesn't notice."

The Ninety-Nine, or T99 for short, was what I called all the kids at our school who shone brightly: the ones who had courage and style. As opposed to the rest, the Twelve Hundred, who were sort of like nameless background characters in the video game of life.

"Have you ever told her that?"

"No. She's afraid of honesty. Everything has to be delicate and indirect."

"I bet she'd want to hear your real feelings. I really bet she would."

Our voices got lower and hazier as we talked about what we'd seen that night. Then, halting, unsure, I mentioned how they'd found me hanging out by myself on those blankets.

"You looked great." His husky voice blew hot air across my neck. "Just totally satisfied with yourself."

"I didn't look, err, sort of lonely?"

"What?" he said. "No! Of course not. The opposite. You were like, *Fuck this party, I'm doing my own thing.*"

I impulsively put an arm out and hugged him close, surrounding myself with the smell of shampoo and soap. "Thank you." I struggled for a better way of putting it. "Thank you."

My eyes closed as a sad woman wailed over the radio. "This song is perfect. . . ." I hummed along quietly, then pitched into a falsetto. I jumped up, grabbing for Dave's hand, and he stared haplessly at me.

"I've never heard this song before."

When he wouldn't get up, I gave a try at flinging my hair and staring at him shyly over my fingertips, like Avani would've done, and Dave didn't seem repulsed. Suddenly I boiled over laughing and flopped down next to him.

"Hey . . . ," he said. "Umm, you seemed kind of upset earlier."

"No. I don't know." My hands covered my face, remembering the college girls I'd run away from the moment things turned weird. "I hate feeling so pathetic."

"Well, if you're pathetic, then what am I?"

"No, no, you're fine. I'll help you." I exhaled and uncovered my face. "You'll learn to ignore that voice."

Now I reached out, took his hands, and my thumb rubbed small circles on his wrist. "You know," I said. "If we were girls, and this was a movie, I'd teach you how to kiss."

He looked away.

"I mean, that's it, right? You're too nervous. But your first kiss . . . you just have to go for it."

Our legs lay on the carpet, and our necks were braced against the bottom of the couch. His chest rose and fell.

"What if she's not into it?"

I nodded. "Well, *some* people say that if you're careful and look real close at her body language, you'll always know. *Other* people say, well, you only go like ninety percent of the way and let her meet you the rest of the way. But, I don't know, this is real life, Dave. People are drunk. They don't know what they want. It's just a fucking kiss. If you get it wrong, she turns away, or she goes really still, and, I don't know, I don't know, I don't know, you feel *so* terrible—I mean—like—every single time I've tried to kiss somebody, my heart's been beating so fast that I could hardly breathe, much less think."

"So . . ." He gulped. "You just go for it."

"Yeah."

We held there for a split second, breathing in sync, and then I touched my lips to his.

His eyes widened, and I had a split-second thought—*Okay, so this is really happening*—before I came close to gagging on

40

the slimy tongue that invaded my mouth. But I held on to that thought, *This is happening, this is happening, this is happening,* and the tongue kept moving around, like some deep-sea tentacle was foraging inside my mouth.

After a few minutes, his hand twisted back and around to go into my pants, and he said, "Is . . . is this okay?"

"We don't have to."

"But I want to."

I wasn't feeling turned on at all, so I tried thinking sexy thoughts, but it was like he was mashing a baked potato down there, so instead I redirected his attention by unzipping his own pants, and I bent down over him.

All through the experience, I kept thinking the weirdest stuff like, *Oh, this is actually not easy* and *What do you do with your teeth?* and *Hmm, this is an interesting experience.* I'd expected Dave to be as turned off as me, but he gasped and moaned, and I was like, *Wait, okay, he's enjoying this. Or maybe he's faking it, because I've definitely done that with Avani. God, she was terrible. So many teeth. Wait, where are my teeth?* And then it was over and I went to the bathroom and used a fair bit of mouthwash.

When I came back, I was afraid he'd want more, but he was sprawled out like a Roman emperor, enthroned on cushions and blankets, and he took my hand with a happy smile. We lay together for a long time.

"That was incredible," he said.

"Yeah," I said. "It was definitely something."

My hand ran along his belly, playing with the little bit of fat around his waist, and he kissed me on the forehead. It was all just very funny, but I didn't laugh.

"You've never done that before?" I said.

"Like that? No. What about you?"

He was still wearing his glasses, and I plucked them off and put them on the table.

"Umm, no," I said. "With girls, I guess, but you're my first guy. It was good, though. Really interesting."

"I, uhh . . ." He rubbed a hand across my chest. "You were awesome."

The oddness overpowered me, and I thought, *Hmm, I'm going to remember this forever. This is actual personal history, being created right here.*

"You don't need to, umm, return the favor." I pointed to myself. "There's no way I could get it up. I'm way too drunk."

"Oh, umm . . ." He smiled. "But . . . maybe some other time?"

"Wow, you're acting *just* like I used to act after Avani went down on me. That's what's *so* funny."

He laughed. "I feel really good."

"Well, yeah. I mean, if you didn't, I'd be offended."

We chatted back and forth, talking about sex, going round and round. He had never come *close* to being with someone else. Never even kissed anyone. And I almost said, *Well, we could keep hooking up if you want*, but instead I yawned. "You can stay the night—my mom won't suspect anything."

And something about that word—"suspect"—broke our trance. He pulled away, sorted out his clothes, and after that we didn't touch each other. He stayed for another hour, but our conversation was awkward and slow, and when he left we did not kiss goodbye.

4

THAT NIGHT I KEPT REMEMBERING his tongue rooting around in my mouth and the oddly similar feeling of spongy foreignness when I'd gone down on him.

In bed I masturbated to the idea of the two of us lying naked on the floor, touching each other, and I was like, *Hmm, so maybe I am the tiniest bit gay*. The night had passed so quickly that I didn't even have a conscious image of his penis to work with, and that actually disappointed me.

Morning announced itself with a headache. My room was windowless and cold—big enough for just a set of shelves and my bed. Originally my mom was gonna sleep there and give me the master bedroom so I'd have more room to study, but one night while she was at the hospital—she's a night nurse in the ICU—I moved all my stuff into this room and wouldn't move out. She earned the money; she deserved the bigger bedroom.

Rolling over, I saw a message.

Dave: Hey, should we talk about last night?

A boundless self-loathing unfurled inside me. I didn't hate what I'd *done* so much as how awkwardly I'd done it. The thought that his brain held the mental image of me dancing and flipping my hair made me want to delete his number and never speak to him again.

My mom rapped on the door for lunch, and when I came out she'd already heated two TV dinners from the Indian store. They have an incredible microwaved tamarind rice that's like two dollars: it's insane. We sat in front of the TV, watching reruns of a popular cop show as we ate.

"Are you ready to start school?"

"Yeah."

"How was your weekend?"

"Great."

"Did you see that girl?"

"No, Mom."

"You're not bringing her here when I'm gone, are you?"

"No."

My mom squinted at me. It'd been a while since her last dye job, so she had a dramatic hint of white that was most visible right at the crown. Her legs were gathered under her, and, for an entirely new level of grossness, her body was swathed in the blanket that Dave and I had lain on.

This was her day off, and she wanted to hang out and catch up—when I was little we used to stay up late, eating popcorn and ice cream and watching TV while she pumped me for gossip about school. Back then I was an outsider, and I didn't really know anything. But at some point last year the gossip got too real—every time we talked, she would get worried—so I'd stopped being honest.

In my room I sent a slew of texts. To Pothan, to Carrie, to Ken. *What's going on tonight?* Every weekend, I relied on them to know what was happening, and I passed the news in turn to people like Dave. Maybe somewhere he had a little Dave of his own who waited on him for crumbs of news.

My heart had quieted. I looked at the rest of the messages from Dave.

Dave: I had a good time.
Dave: Are you gonna text me? Are things weird now?

Each message shot a pang through my stomach.

Me: Hey, no need to talk. That was something I'd sort of wanted to do—I mean to someone, not necessarily to you!—for a little while. So it's totally fine.

I paused for a few seconds. That was . . . not untrue. I'd wondered what it'd be like to be with a guy. And I'd discovered it was okay; nothing special.

Dave: Oh, wow. I didn't know that about you.

Me: How could you? I've literally never told a single soul about it.

Dave: Well I'm honored, and you know I'm totally cool with whatever you are.

Dave: Or want to be.

Dave: Wow, I'm being super awkward right now.

Me: So you've really never thought about being with another guy?

Dave: Honestly, no. That was a total surprise.

Me: Oh, okay.

Me: You seemed into it.

Dave: I was! But things happened really fast.

I blinked a few times.

Me: Yeah, totally.

Dave: Lol. Hey, what's going on tonight? You want to hang out?

To be honest I didn't. But I'd learned from Avani that the more you *let* it be awkward, the more awkward it actually gets.

Me: Yeah, let's do it. Hey, you're still into Mari, right? You should test your newly found move-making skills out on her!

Dave: Oh, umm, well actually she's been texting me about you. She wants the three of us to do something. Maybe see the new Avengers movie? I think she really liked you.

Me: Would it be weird to have me along?

Dave: I don't know. I think I totally screwed things up with her last night. Her and I are probably done.

Me: Dave!

Dave: Nandan!

Me: Do you want it to be done?

Dave: I'm not sure. At this point I'm a little tired of it.

Me: But you like her.

Dave: Well I don't want to marry her.

Dave: But I mean you saw her. She's really cool. I don't know. I honestly try not to think about it.

Me: Then don't. Just let me handle it.

The more I considered it, the more I wanted to intervene directly with Dave and Mari.

Just giving advice wasn't working. Like, I could wait for Dave to make a move on his own, but that would probably never happen. The fact is, you need confidence in order to get girls, but the most confident guys are assholes. People don't decide to be nervous, nerdy guys like Dave. Their nervousness comes from the realization that it's fundamentally sort of weird to think some random girl would want to kiss you.

Obviously what you'd want is for guys to pay attention, read the signs, watch her body language, and intuit when she's into it. But that's next-level shit. In order to do that, you need to get it wrong a bunch of times, and guys like Dave would be shattered after a few failures.

Which is why he needed my help, because from what I could see Mari was *clearly* into Dave—you don't hang out with someone in a date-like way for hours upon hours, day after day, unless you're desperate for them to make a move—and the two of them just needed the smallest possible nudge to get them together.

But I couldn't do it alone. If I went with them by myself, then just by hanging around, unattached on my own, I'd make Mari feel weird about moving things forward with Dave. We needed a fourth wheel.

Avani got back to me within an hour.

Avani: What's up? Where'd you go last night? People were looking for you.
Me: Dave drove me home.
Me: Actually, he's the reason I'm texting.
Me: I've got a scheme I want to involve you in.
Avani: Uhh, I don't know if I like the sound of that. . . .

Me: Come on, it'll be fun. You always say you're gonna embark upon schemes with me.

Avani: Do I say that?

Me: What're you up to right now? Can I come over?

Avani: Doing my nails.

Me: Lol, such a girl.

Avani: Hey, that was a microaggression.

Me: Whatever, keep your cissexism to yourself.

Avani: I meant it was a microaggression because the term hewed to the gender binary.

Me: I hewed your mom last night.

Avani: Gross.

Me: Ageist.

Our school was *hella* liberal, and we'd had assemblies on all the politically correct terminology. Avani loved to make fun of it all, but you could tell she sort of believed in it.

Me: Come on. Just to hang out. And anyway I'm bored.

Avani: Sigh. Fine. Don't ring the bell.

I walked into the hills. Biking would've been faster, but I might've been seen. Everybody walked sometimes, but only people without cars still used bikes.

The day was warm and incredible, with a pale blue sky, and the breeze ruffled the hair on my bare legs and arms. Part of me was insanely, deliriously excited at the idea of being alone with Avani. Surely that was far from queer? I'd never felt like that about seeing Dave. This girl had always keyed me up, right from the beginning.

Avani's basement was filled with pinball machines. As a hobby, her dad purchased them from all over the country, restored them in his garage, hauled them into the basement, and then never ever used them.

Her cat rubbed himself against my shins. When I picked him up, Lucifer went completely inert, turning into a purring mass of fur.

I ducked under the lit-up neon beer sign (another project of her dad's) and saw Avani on the couch. The television was on but quiet: she was watching *RuPaul's Drag Race* with her earbuds plugged into the remote control.

Avani did have a bedroom somewhere above us in the house, but I'd never seen it. She and I always hung out in her subterranean lair.

I crept up on her, still holding the cat. Avani wore a flannel shirt and black sweatpants. Her feet were propped on the table, and she applied a layer of base coat as Ru scolded one of the drag queens for her laziness.

"Hey, I'm here," I said. Avani laid down another clear stripe.

The cat squealed, and I set him on the ground. Lucifer got spooked, dashing across the carpet.

Avani startled me with a shout: "NANDAN."

"I'm right behind you."

"NANDAN, ARE YOU HERE? DON'T HIDE FROM ME."

This was okay in her basement, but she did this at school too: Whenever her earbuds were in, she shouted. Not a good trait for a gossip to have. Secrets had definitely been spilled that way.

I sat on my music stool, which was kitty-corner to the sofa. She knocked her head from side to side.

"NANDAN. HELP."

She actually wanted me to take out her earbuds.

"NANDAN, I DON'T WANT MY FINGERNAILS ANYWHERE NEAR MY HAIR."

She swiveled her head, trying to catch the earbud cord between her neck and her shoulder. I grabbed the cord, jerking it from both ears at once.

"Yay," she said without looking up. "And now . . ."

I paused the show too.

"Thanks."

"Sure."

"You mad?"

"At what?"

"Did I emasculate you? Was that emasculating? My mom said today I have a naturally strong personality, and I shouldn't worry about emasculating men, and I didn't, until she said that, but now I do."

Avani was very light skinned: if it wasn't for her name, you might not even know she was Indian. Her hair was large and so voluminous—much larger than her head—and was a dark, rich black, with the tiniest hint of brown. Her sister once drew a picture of her that was just a stick figure with a river of black hair that trailed down from the head and wrapped, like Lady Godiva's, around her whole body.

She ran the brush over her pinky toe.

"So what's up?"

"I don't know." I wedged myself into the L of her couch. "Can't we just hang out?"

"Suuuuuuure we can."

Dave's words came into my mind. *Tell her your real feelings.* "Avani," I said. "Last year you were always complaining about Lyle Brashear and his parties. You wanted something different. Something better. But this year it's exactly the same."

Lyle was the king of last year's Ninety-Nine. He was Pothan times a thousand: Where Pothan was good-natured and willing to let you have fun, so long as you accepted his dominance, Lyle needed to be in control of everything at all times. The moment Lyle rolled into a party, it'd inevitably become mean and dangerous and, worst of all, completely boring.

She looked over her shoulder at me. "So?"

"Okay, okay, okay," I said. "This is going to sound so nerdy, but bear with me. . . . There is this thing I call the Ninety-Nine. . . ."

Her pale green eyes drank up my theories, and she listened

53

for ten minutes without laughing as I explained everything, including my theory that Avani and Pothan were in a bitter struggle for the soul of the Ninety-Nine and right now she was losing.

I told her that Pothan stood for noise and mess and outrage and drunkenness. When you spent a night with Pothan, you didn't remember anything you said, all you remembered was the trail of adventure and destruction. Pothan wasn't about words—although he could talk when he needed to—he was about that wordless-grunting thing that formed between guys when they came together in a soup of drunkenness and loneliness. He stood for nights that were edgy and dangerous, but also weirdly formless and without expectations.

Avani on the other hand wasn't any weaker or gentler, but she stood for something different. When you were with Avani, you were always on your guard. Every word counted. Every gesture mattered. Every interaction was watched and commented upon. Avani was all about words. She wanted long, breezy nights when packs of girls stood around, drinking and chatting and gossiping and bonding, while packs of guys were shoved to the edges of the party, simmering, until they figured out how to somehow break into the girl groups. Nights when you maybe hooked up if a guy stepped in and proved himself to you, but when you didn't *need* to. Nights when it'd be just as fun and just as cool to end up on your best friend's bed, debriefing about who had or hadn't kissed whom.

This wasn't totally about guys and girls. Carrie was more in Pothan's camp, for one thing, as the Roman candles had demonstrated, but Carrie was queer, and maybe that made a difference. I wasn't sure.

Looking at Avani sitting there with her toes splayed out in front of her and the overhead lights catching the faint brown highlights in her black hair, a sense of longing filled my chest. She had something that I wanted so badly.

You could *say* gender roles weren't real or didn't matter, but we still lived in a world where they existed. My heart belonged 100 percent with Avani and with her vision of the world, but she wouldn't accept me into the fold, whereas Pothan just *assumed* I was with him. The thing is, you can't just "be yourself," if whenever people look at you they see something entirely different.

"It's like a war, Avani," I said. And she was right on the verge of laughing and saying something cutting, something about how I was taking this way too seriously, when I smiled and pulled back. "And of course it's not a big deal. In two years, none of us will care about this. But right now, at this moment, this is important. Like, don't pretend you're not sitting here feeling lonely because Carrie won't watch *Drag Race* with you anymore. Well, you can keep hiding, or you can do something about it."

That got her. She jolted upright with one middle toe still only half painted. "People grow up," she said.

"That's Carrie talking," I said. "That's not you. Breaking things and vomiting on the beach isn't grown. This"—I waved my arm—"this is grown."

"A basement full of vintage pinball machines?"

"No, I'm talking about this, us, being real, being—"

She let out a large breath. "Nandan, I don't know." The corner of her mouth turned down. "I keep thinking maybe I shouldn't go out anymore. But even Jessie gets bored sometimes. And so do I! Sometimes I think maybe I should've made better friends."

"No, Avani," I said. "I've been on the beach with you, and I've seen what happens there. It's *not* fun. We can do better."

Her chest rose slowly. "All right. How?"

"Ummmmmmmmmmm . . ." I drew out the word, happy to be here, in this basement, dancing on the edge of success. "You . . . could help me set up Dave with this girl."

Her lower eyelids had red smudges from too little sleep. "Why would I do that?"

"I don't know. It'll be fun. It's—it's—it's a caper. Come on. There's nobody else who'd be good for this. It'll be a story. Aaaaaaaand it'll show Carrie that *you* can have fun too."

I explained it all to her, a little haltingly, trying to emphasize how little time it'd take and how *nothing* else was happening tonight.

"Mmmm." She tucked a strand of hair behind her ear. "Okay."

"Really?"

"Sure, yeah, what's the plan?"

"They're going to a movie. We'll invite ourselves along and nudge them in the right direction."

"Going to the movies together. I love it. Which theater? Let's go to the Century 20 at Redwood City and then to Tartine. It'll be like being thirteen again."

She got mixed up about Dave and thought he was a sophomore. When I said he was our year, I barely stopped myself from adding, *Oh yeah, and by the way, I hooked up with him last night.*

Avani scanned through her phone, looking for a third person. "You know who'd be really good for this? Hen."

"Come on," I said. "Can't we just invite Carrie?"

I said that I hardly knew Henry—his number wasn't even in my phone!—and after some wrangling, Avani agreed to text Carrie instead; I texted Dave to get him on board too.

While we were waiting for their responses, I watched Avani put together her face. This was a new experience; at the beach or at parties she always showed up fully formed. But now, as she used a variety of pens and brushes, her eyes blossomed, her skin turned smooth, and every feature got bigger and sharper.

"This is nice," I said. "I wish there was something I could do too. Like a . . . a . . . a preparatory thing. So we could get ready together. You know, like your guys', umm, homecoming tea party."

"You remember that?" she said.

Last year before homecoming Avani had invited Carrie and Jessie over for a long afternoon of drinking tea and doing their nails and hair. Strictly a sober occasion, since they wouldn't let you into the dance if you were drunk. That meant, too, that her and their parents could be involved, and apparently all the families had a really nice time together.

Of course afterward we changed plans at the last minute and went to Lyle Brashear's party instead of actually going to homecoming. But I still remembered when the three of them had come to pick us up in the limo Avani's dad had rented. They had seemed so happy and proud and beautiful, and I'd envied them for being a unit, a group, a conjoined six-legged monster that always walked the earth together, no matter what.

"I really, really wanted to be there."

"You wouldn't have liked it."

"I don't know, Avani. I like a lot of things."

Actually, I'd gotten excited by the idea of Carrie coming along. It'd be really cool for her and me and Avani to hang out together. Maybe we could invite Jessie too.

Her phone chimed. "Carrie can't make it. Now can you talk to Hen?"

"Fine. Umm, let me use your phone."

I called him. Using my voice. In real time. He was surprised to discover it was really me, and at first said he was busy, but Avani whispered, "Tell him you need his help."

"One second." I put the phone on mute and hissed. "Can't you do the talking? He and I really aren't friends."

"Tell him you need his help. Tell him the plan."

"Uhh, okay."

I stuttered my way through an explanation, feeling brutally stupid, and in the few seconds after finishing, I was sure nobody would ever agree to do this. There was silence on the phone, and I kept talking. "Okay, it's sort of weird, but I dunno, I want to do something that's not, like, 'get drunk at the beach,' 'get drunk in a basement,' 'get drunk in a car parked in a field next to a cliff.'"

"Wait, where's this cliff? I want to see the cliff."

"Just drive down Skyline and look for all the smashed bottles."

"So . . . everywhere on Skyline. Everywhere."

I laughed. Hen was one of those guys who always had a witty comment, and I told myself that guys like him needed straight men (LOL) to set up their punch lines, but I secretly wished I could be the funny one sometimes.

"Look, you're high up on the list for this caper, but I can find someone else."

"Now it's a caper. Is there an actual plan of some sort?"

"Yeah. Improvise."

"Okay. You'll pick me up?"

"Definitely."

"And pay for my ticket?"

"Mmm, sure."

"And snacks?"

"I'll pay for everything."

"Wait, who's getting set up with whom?" Avani broke in.

My ears went red. "Uhh, cool, see you soon, bye."

When the call ended, she pinched my cheek. "You got so embarrassed. You're uncomfortable around Hen. You need to work on that." When she let go, I rubbed my face. Seeing her there, smiling at me, I thought about confessing to my hookup with Dave. I knew she'd accept and love me, and it'd be cool, and probably afterward we'd even be closer. But then I saw the sweep of her body on the couch, and I thought, *How can I tell her I'm gay when really she is the person I think about all the time?*

But still the pressure to be honest only dissipated when she flicked a switch and RuPaul's face unfroze and began once more to speak.

5

AVANI MADE US STOP FOR coffee—not Starbucks, it had to be Philz—so we were twenty minutes late even before we started. The coffee was a stream of acid poured directly into my tense stomach, but I drank it just to have something to do. I'd thought our outing would be full of laughter and jokes, but Avani spent most of the coffee break on her phone, texting with Jessie.

After we got back into the car, I kept saying I couldn't believe this thing had come together. Finally she said, "Please stop saying 'caper.' I never want to hear that word again."

"What if we decide to get bagels?"

"Then say you want them with those tiny pickled olive things. Just don't say caper, or I'm kicking you out of the car."

When we picked up Hen, the awkwardness multiplied. My brain still ached from the drinking on the beach, and I kept running out of things to say. Even before we arrived, the car stank of boredom and regret.

The mall was immense, tree covered, and mostly open to the air. Flowering vines hung from the mezzanines above, and the staircases and promenades curved around each other to catch maximum sunlight.

We huddled in a corner of the food court. Hen and Avani were hardly talking, and certainly not to each other. When Avani whipped out her phone, it was actually a relief to not have to entertain her anymore.

Dave bounded up, smiling. He was back in his bow tie, and I had the urge to ruffle his hair. Despite everything, my mouth cranked into a smile, and something inside me relaxed. He and I at least were totally natural around each other.

"Hey," I said.

"Nice, nice," he said. "Happy to see everybody." The sunlight brought out the many different tones of his skin, and all of them were radiant. "Hey, have you bought your tickets yet? Mari's not here yet, but I'm gonna buy hers."

He hardly looked at Hen or Avani, and instead buzzed around my left side, asking if I'd ever seen these movies, which of course left the other two off by themselves, struggling to talk.

I could tell they were dying inside, and if only I was a better person—somebody stronger, more confident and interesting—I would've used our time in line to crack jokes and bring us together, but instead we waited in silence.

The first show was sold out, so we had to buy tickets for an hour later. We stood in line for smoothies, then sat languidly in the food court, right in the sun, because all the shady tables were taken, and Avani abandoned us immediately, glomming onto a nearby group of girls, standing over them chatting and smiling while the three of us stared helplessly.

"Do you know them?" I said.

"No," Hen said.

"I don't think they go to our school."

"They could."

"Well they're not in the, uhh"—Dave looked at me—"the Ninety-Nine."

My eyes widened. Although I loved that term, it also embarrassed me. I didn't want Hen to know I thought about that stuff. But Henry was lost inside the phone on his lap.

I spotted Mari first and waved urgently at her. Her footsteps were short but quick, and she threw open her arms, crashing into me. "Oh, hey! You again!" Then she slid into the bench.

Looking at our drinks, she said, "Wait, I should get a smoothie too." Just as quickly, she hopped up and stood by herself.

Both Hen and I looked at Dave.

"Well . . . ?" Hen said.

"Uhh, yeah, you should go with her," I whispered.

"Wouldn't that be awkward?" Dave said.

"It's more awkward to sit here."

"And buy it for her!" Hen whispered loudly. As Dave left, Hen batted his eyelashes at me. "Straight girls love that, right?"

"Doesn't everybody? I mean you liked when I bought your ticket, right?"

"Yeah, but only in the way I like free stuff. Not in an extra 'confirming our respective gender roles' way."

I inspected Hen's perfect face. I didn't feel anything for him. I imagined him naked, imagined the two of us together, and it wasn't gross or anything, but then I looked at Avani, standing half in the sunlight and half out, with her bare legs shining, and her image tugged at my eyes and at my heart in a way that Hen's body couldn't match.

Hen was still tapping at his phone, and I was still mired in dread. Nothing would save this situation. It was beyond awkward. I needed to say or do something immediately.

"Uhh," I said. "You're really funny. That was funny, the gender-roles thing."

He looked up, his eyebrows quirking a little bit. "Thanks," he said. "That's nice."

"Well . . . are you gonna say something nice about me?"

"Hmm . . . I . . . ." His eyes dropped, then rose. "I like your pants."

I looked at my shorts, which were bright orange. "Really? That's what you're going with?"

"You have very good taste in pants. Not just these ones. Many of your pants are excellent."

"Hmm, but not my shirts."

"No, very average, the shirts."

He said this completely deadpan, and his face didn't twitch even when I laughed. I took half a breath, expecting him to loosen up, but his eyes returned to his phone. I wanted to snatch it up and smash it on the ground. Hen's cleverness was actually a burden on everybody else: he relied on us to provide the setup for these clever jabs that systematically disrupted the flow of conversation.

"Who're you texting?"

"Oh—" He put down his phone. "Nobody."

"What?" I said. "A crush?"

"Uhhh, no. It's my brother."

His angry tone surprised me. "Did I say something wrong?"

"N-no." He shrugged. "You're fine."

"Hey, uhh, how—" I stopped. Hen hated that question: *How did you know you were gay?* He always asked, *How did you know you were straight?* Which I thought was stupid, because lots of people *didn't* know they were straight.

"So . . ." My mouth made an O. "Last night I might've hooked up with a guy."

Hen's eyes narrowed. "Hmm . . . what exactly are we talking about? A kiss?"

"I might possibly have gone down on him."

"Nandan!" he said. "Whoa!"

"Quiet," I said. "Jesus."

65

"Sorry. But I really wasn't expecting you to say that."

Now his voice was almost too low. In the distance Avani looked up as her social sensors registered the slight change in dynamic at our table.

"What'd you think it would be?" I said.

"I don't know. That you lost a bet and had to make out with Ken? Oh my God . . . was it Ken?"

I laughed, but he didn't blink.

"So it wasn't Ken," he said.

"No."

"Wait, okay, I'm gonna be cool. So . . . how do you feel about it?"

"I am . . . perhaps exploring the notion of becoming gay."

He slapped me on the wrist. "You are so funny. Now who was it? Come on. Was it somebody I know?"

My eyes flicked to the corner, and Henry turned to see Dave and Mari coming back. As the two sat down, Hen gave me a huge, gape-jawed expression, then mouthed a word I couldn't make out.

Dave sat down next to me and Mari sat next to Hen. "Sssssssssooooooooo," Hen said. "How's the smoothie?"

"What's going on?" Mari said.

"Hen and I were talking about some personal stuff." I shrugged.

He rolled his eyes. "Mari," he said. "You and Dave, an item or no?"

"Uhh, what?"

"Dave," Hen said. "What're your intentions toward this nice lady here?"

My friend bowed his shoulders inward, shrinking away from us. "Errr . . ."

"Nandan," Hen said. "You're the instigator of this caper. What say you?"

"Uhhh . . . ," I said.

Mari mouthed a question: *Caper?*

"Typical," Hen said. "No follow-through. And now there's only silence."

"Well I think they have to answer for themselves," I said.

"You two"—Henry snapped his fingers—"you both like video games, yes?"

Mari was red. "Yeah. Sure."

"Good. There's a GameStop." He pointed. "Go to the GameStop. Hold hands. Decide if you like each other. If you don't, that's totally fine. But if you do, please kiss before coming back, so you can put us out of our misery."

Dave looked at him.

I shrugged. "Sounds good to me."

Now all the heads turned to Mari, and she hopped up, her eyes laughing, and put out a hand. "Come on. I guess those are the orders."

Once she was gone, I said, "See, that's the kind of thing I couldn't ever do."

"What're you talking about?" he said. "I don't see why straight guys can't be awesome. Y'all just choose not to be."

"No, from me that'd be creepy or weird."

"What's weird is you and Dave hooked up!" he said. "That's mind-blowing."

"Yeah. I don't know. I was drunk."

"Was *he* drunk?"

"No." I shook my head. "But he wasn't very into it."

"He said that?"

"No, but afterward it got weird. And he said that hooking up with guys wasn't even on his radar."

Hen let out a long sigh. "The straight guys. We can have them for a night, but no more."

"Yeah . . . ," I said. "I guess."

"You," Hen said. "I would not have guessed you. I'd have thought Ken maybe. Or Niko."

"Niko! You know him?"

"Of course. Everybody knows Niko."

"I *need* to meet him."

Henry can't keep it serious for long, so we laughed and made fun of Niko and ourselves. And right at the moment when he reached forward to touch the back of my hand, I looked at Avani and witnessed one of the most awesome things I'd ever beheld—I *saw* the force of Hen and me, laughing and connecting, pull her back toward us. The motion was slow and unwilling, she was like an iron ball wobbling between two powerful magnets, but all of a sudden she said goodbye to the girls and made her way back to us.

She came back. "Sorry, guys. Some Holy Redeemer girls I hadn't seen in a while. Rachel was telling an incredible story—"

"We were talking about Niko Diamandis!" Without thinking, I dropped that into the conversation before Hen could ask about the incredible story. Hen filled her in, and when she tried to redirect the conversation to herself—she said her friend Rachel was dating a guy who—

"See!" I interrupted. "Not everybody has heard of Niko."

"Well, of course *Avani* hasn't," Hen said. "She's such a princess."

"Hey."

"It's not an insult, it's a descriptor. You're a very pretty princess, don't worry. It's just that you wouldn't ever go for a guy who wears a fanny pack."

"Eww, who would?"

"Only like half the school, honey."

"'Honey,' that's bold," I said. "I've never heard you call someone 'honey.'"

"I feel very called-out right now," Hen said. "I'm allowed to test-drive some new expressions once in a while."

That wasn't the end. The conversation was intense and nerve-racking. I didn't have a second to think: I was operating solely by instinct, rushing in to stop Avani from going off on some self-absorbed tangent that would kill Hen's brief and partial interest in her. But finally the moment approached for the movie, and I saw Avani look at her phone, and I *knew* that she was about to bail on us, and my heart was hammering so loudly, because on some level that would ruin everything, so I finally got her back onto Rachel's story.

"Well, okay," Avani said. "Rachel was, like, driving down University, and a strange guy got into her car—wait, okay so for context, Rachel drives a really expensive electric car—it's always running out of batteries, and she'll have to look around for a Whole Foods, because they have these charging stations, and then we'll be trapped at Whole Foods, just sort of chilling in the parking lot and—"

I let her go on for a bit, then said, "Oh, wait, it's time for the movie," and she, unwilling to cut her story short, followed us all the way to the theater, where we saw Mari and Dave, flushed and happy, hurriedly drop each other's hands.

"Hey," I whispered to Hen. "Let's see if we can get these two to sit together, but, like, in front of us."

"I'll scout out seats."

"Wait, yes, this is great."

He went ahead to find seats while the rest of us got snacks, and when we finally got in, there were three seats in the middle and two seats right ahead. It was a little awkward, but Mari and Dave bumbled into the seats.

I sat between Hen and Avani, and as the trailers began, he poked me in the side and said, "What's our next move?"

"I don't know," I whispered. "We're not sure if they've kissed yet."

Avani dropped into our conversation. "What's going on?"

Mari looked back, and the three of us went silent.

"Shouldn't he, like, put his arm around her?" Hen said.

We looked at the two of them.

"How do we make this happen?" I said.

"Oh my God, this is agonizing," Hen said.

"I'm thinking they should've sat in back of us," I said. "I think they're embarrassed to have us watching."

"Agh, yes, you're right."

"You guys." Avani rolled her eyes. She leaned forward, her hair brushing Dave's shoulder, and whispered in his ear. He looked back but didn't move. She whispered again.

Slowly, creakily, his arm swung up and over the back of the seat, where it stayed, completely not in contact with Mari's body at all. Hen and I barely suppressed hysterical giggles, and, shortly after the movie started, Hen took Dave's fingers, pulled them off the back of the seat and affixed them to Mari's shoulder.

When we came out, the two nerds were arguing over the movie, and we three watched them from ten feet away like proud parents.

"Do we leave them?" I said.

"I want them to be holding hands," Henry said. "Make them be holding hands."

"But can we really make them?"

Avani rolled her eyes again. Then she went to Dave and whispered in his ear again. He reached down and took Mari's hand, but he paired the gesture with a deadly glare at Hen and me. Mari simultaneously grew taller and frailer, as if her increased size was catching the wind and hampering her ability to move.

"Now how do we make them kiss?" Hen said.

"I don't know," I said. "It's the ultimate question."

"Maybe I just push their faces together."

"That probably would be a bad—"

"I was joking!" he said. "I thought you said I was funny."

"Honestly . . ." I shook my head. "I don't know. I've given Dave some coaching on how to make a move. Just let our little chickee open his wings and fly."

"I'll bet you coached him," Hen said.

Now I narrowed my eyes at him, but the joke steadied me. I liked that Hen was treating this as exciting rather than strange.

They wandered a few steps ahead, and we were ready to just sneak off, but then Mari stopped, and she looked back, waiting for us, so Hen and I hurried to catch up.

"Umm," she said. "Do, umm, does anyone want ice cream?"

Hen and Avani and I looked at each other. "Well, we, uhh . . . we actually drove together . . . and . . . err . . ."

It was Hen who broke through the stuttering. "I really do have to go home."

"Yeah, I guess the two of us ought to go too."

"But . . . oh, but . . . what did you think of the movie?"

Dave dropped Mari's hand, and she unconsciously rubbed it.

"It was . . . good," Avani said.

"Boring," Henry said. "Very boring. So boring. The most boring thing I've ever been bored by."

"Oh . . ."

"Don't mind him," I said. "He's joking."

"No, I wasn't," Hen said. "It was awful."

"Umm . . . ," I said. "I, uhh, I liked it. Thanks for persuading us to go, Dave."

"Oh yeah!" Avani said. "Thanks, dude."

Hen caught on. "Yeah. Thanks. The movie was terrible, but this was a cultural experience. You're not uncool, Bow Tie."

With each compliment, Dave swelled up a little. And he started to talk animatedly about the movie.

"And now we must go," Hen said. "But hold on a moment: did you two happen to kiss?"

Mari flushed and drew closer to Dave. Hen delivered a pitch-perfect wink.

"Okay, so now we're leaving you alone," he said. "And we'd like you very much to explore the idea of kissing some more, because I have plans next weekend, and I don't have time to do this again."

In the car, the three of us hashed and rehashed the experience.

73

There was a loud debate on whether Avani or Hen had been more awkward in the "put your arm around her shoulder" saga.

Hen kept saying, "But the drama. The simple human drama. Riveting."

We were stopped outside my house—I was closest to the theater—for a good half hour. I was on the verge of asking if they wanted to hang out more, but, finally, I got out and let them drive away.

6

ALL NIGHT I RESISTED THE urge to text Avani and Hen. Something about that evening, I thought, had forged us into a unit. And I had guided every moment of it. These people hadn't *wanted* to go out and they hadn't wanted to hang out, but I'd asked the right questions, infusing them with my own energy, and everything had worked!

Except now my stomach ached whenever I thought about texting them. Because everything could fall apart so easily. One unanswered text will hang forever between you and another person. Every time they look at your name in their phone, they'll remember that time you wanted some recognition from them and they didn't give it, and they'll always have this feeling that they're better than you. That you're a pest.

Henry broke the silence by DMing me on Instagram.

Henry: Hey, Nandan, this is you, right?

I was lying on my bed, watching YouTube videos, and I didn't even think about playing it cool.

Me: Yep, it's me!
Henry: Hey!
Henry: Dude, thanks for coming out to me earlier. I mean it was a weird moment, but that definitely felt like a coming-out.

My face broke out in sweat.

Me: Lol, maybe.
Me: You're not gonna tell anyone, right?
Henry: No no, of course not.
Henry: Who do you think I am?
Henry: I just wanted to text and say I'm available to talk.
Henry: Oh, also, how do you feel?!
Me: About what?
Henry: About seeing Dave with a girl. I mean we didn't really get to talk much. Lol, I feel stupid.

Seeing Henry type "Lol" was the most disturbing thing that had happened all day. I felt like the guy was disintegrating in front of my eyes. I quickly turned things around, asking if *he* was okay, and that opened up an immense flood of feelings on his part. He said I wasn't the first guy who had confessed to him that they might have gay feelings, but I was the first person who'd actually *done* anything about it. All the other guys had been so coy, so shy, and so scared, and they would tell Hen, and then later they'd deny it, or say it was a joke, or they were confused, or they weren't ready to be out.

Henry: But when you told me about you and Dave

Henry: And it was soooo casual

Henry: I almost died.

Me: I'm definitely not hung up on Dave.

Henry: No, and don't think you and me need to do any-thing.

Henry: Actually, it's so awkward. Have you ever thought that if you came out publicly, and I'm not saying you would ever do that or are prepared for that, then pretty much everyone would expect you and me to get together? Or at least to consider it.

I was about to shoot him a bland "haha" but I stopped myself. Somewhere on the other side of my phone was a real person, typing desperately, and I wanted to get out of this conversation as quickly as possible, with as little damage as possible, but I couldn't—not without hurting Hen.

Me: I guess you're right.

Henry: Not that I'm saying we would.

Me: Yeah, I'm not sure I'm ready for that.

Henry: I might not even like you. But it's something I've thought about. The other gay guy—who would it be? who would take my crown?—Nandan, you weren't even on my radar.

Me: What? But you always seemed as if you liked me!

Henry: Yes, but not in a "you tripped my gaydar" sort of way.

Henry: Because you didn't. At all.

Me: Not even with my pants?

Henry: Maybe the pants should've been a warning.

We joked for a few more minutes, and then Henry abruptly turned serious. He said he was jealous of me. He'd never hooked up with anyone—never so much as kissed another guy—and sometimes he watched these teen TV shows about guys finding boyfriends even in high school, and he just loathed both himself and the TV shows so much, because he didn't even know how to *start*. Well he did—he could lie about his age—go on Tinder or Grindr—he had done that a time or two, and seen lots of guys—but it felt so sleazy, and he didn't want it to be like that!

I joked that he just needed to make a move on some shy guy like Dave, and Henry said he couldn't—the embarrassment would be too much, he would just die—and I said that's weird, that's exactly the problem Dave had—and—and—and this is why I sort of thought I wasn't gay, because kissing Dave was only a joke, and doing that other stuff was only a test.

He asked, "Err, this is awkward, but can you tell me what it was like?"

So I described going down on Dave as best as I could remember, and the conversation wasn't too sexy, just clinical and informative, and Henry asked lots of questions, and we made jokes to ease the tension, and we spiraled onward enjoyably, for hour after hour, through many drinks of water and whiskey and several bowls of popcorn, right until two a.m., when, my eyes dark and heavy, he finally let me go to sleep.

The next day I almost texted Henry again, but I was scared it'd turn into another marathon gabfest, and although part of me wanted that, another part couldn't quite handle it. Besides, after two days of neglect, my usual life was begging for attention.

Dave wrote to say that things had gone okay with him and Mari.

Me: Awesome! You're amazing.
Dave: I didn't *do* anything.
Me: So what? It's great.
Dave: Yeah, sure. Well, thanks. Hey, uhh, Mari and I are going to another movie tonight, if you want to come.
Me: Lol, no time. Besides, you don't need me anymore.

Pothan and Ken and I went out almost every day and every night during the last week of summer. Pothan filled me with advice, and I talked to a dozen different girls, hooking up with one—my first since Avani—and finding, to my surprise, that it was totally okay, especially because she didn't, thank God, expect me to have sex with her. Not that I wasn't into that! Just—it's a lot of pressure, the first time you've met someone. Although if things are headed that way, then you don't want to make things weird by holding off.

Wherever we went, Pothan clapped me on the shoulder, saying I was "a natural. Just a goddamn natural," while Avani stood aloof in her sunglasses, usually with Jessie and some other girls. On occasion, Carrie hung with them, but more often they ignored each other. Avani and I talked a few times, but our realest conversation was late one night over text.

Me: All right, we need to plan more tiny pickled olive thingies.

Avani: What?

Me: You won't let me use the word.

Avani: Lol, you're crazy.

Me: Come on, admit it, that was really fun.

Avani: Okay, but where do we go now?

Me: Invite us to the lake house over Labor Day weekend!

Me: I won't let Ken and Pothan divert me this time.

Avani: Yeah, I don't know. The only useful thing Lyle

Brashear ever taught me was that throwing parties isn't worth it. People don't respect you. They just come in and take advantage of you.

Me: But this won't be a party. It'll be chill, like your weekends up there with Carrie and Jessie.

Avani: Yeah. I don't know.

Me: I bet Carrie will come if she knows me and Dave and Hen are going.

It was the wrong thing to say. Avani drifted away from the conversation, but I waited for my moment to bring it up again. A weekend that would be chill. No drinking. Or less drinking. Not so relentlessly focused on hooking up or struggling for dominance or maintaining the illusion that your life was perfect. A weekend when we'd just have fun and get closer. Because that was the weird thing about Ken and Pothan: even after a whole summer, I hardly knew them at all.

As the week continued, my hangovers stacked up, carrying over from day to day, and I always had an unsettled stomach and dry eyes and a light, continuous headache. But even the shitty feeling became a bonding experience; Ken and Pothan laughed every time I complained and laughed harder when I vomited.

"I think I'm literally dying," I said as I groaned in the back seat of the car.

"Dude," Pothan said. "I felt exactly the same way last summer. Lyle was so goddamn hard on us. But it'll get easier."

"Every cell in my brain is screaming in silent torment."

"Where we going tonight?" Ken said.

"Umm . . . Jessie's?" Pothan said.

"'Kay. Do we need more booze?" Ken asked.

"Nah, I'm tired of spending money. Let's see what she's got."

"Please," I said. "No more alcohol."

I stumbled into the next party and went directly to the nearest bottle of liquor. Even the smell of alcohol almost made me vomit, but I mixed the vodka with some orange juice I found in the fridge, and the screwdriver sizzled through my limbs and heart.

Instead of rejoining the Pothan-and-Ken show, I sat on the back deck next to a few kids huddling over a single phone and put my head into my hands.

Henry had texted a few times, and I had texted back, but always hurriedly, saying I was headed out. For some reason I couldn't bear to talk to him. We'd shared too much, gone too deep, and any further talking would make it even weirder. Honestly I was already halfway afraid to go out to parties for fear he'd be there. The situation sickened me. I was destroying my new friendship with Henry. And for no reason other than shame and fear.

We were underneath large yellow floodlights that gave a devilish look to every face. The quietness of the night was interrupted by squeaks and creaks from the wooden deck. And all around me the chatter rose and fell like the breathing of a living organism.

I looked over the sweep of people, their hands and feet moving slowly, orienting and reorienting, bodies shifting to block out some people and moving to accept others, and I instantly saw that this party was a good one. Not sick, not desperate, not too much tilted in favor of craziness. And not full of that aura of stunted violence that Lyle used to bring to parties last year.

Maybe I wasn't a leader, like Lyle or Pothan or Avani. But I didn't have to be a follower either. That afternoon at the mall, I'd seen a third way—not leader and not follower, but something different, separate, and yet still valued. People didn't need to particularly like me. They didn't need to glow with the energy of my presence. They didn't need to seek out my friendship. Instead I could be a spider, sitting alone, spinning my own webs, making my own little plans that I carried out with the occasional help of people who were much bigger and braver than me.

Suddenly Ken and Pothan were around me.

"Dude, didn't you get my texts?" Pothan said. "We're leaving."

"What?"

"Yeah, this party sucks."

"Uhh, no, it's fine. It's good."

"There's nobody here. Nothing is happening."

I looked up, frowning. "That is plainly not true."

"We're headed to the beach. Come on. Carrie's there. She's got more fireworks. It's supposed to be epic."

"Dude."

"Come on."

It took me some time, in my drunk and sick state, to explain that I wasn't coming. Pothan asked what the fuck was I pulling—I didn't even have a car; they were my ride—and I said, "Whatever, Avani will give me a ride home."

"I don't think she's even here."

"Of course she's here. This is Jessie's party."

The argument went on and on and on, and finally I yelled at them to just *leave*, and I ran inside, found a toilet, and forced myself to puke. Afterward, sipping water from the sink, feeling pale and twitchy, I saw that Pothan had texted me.

Pothan: Whatever, we're going to the beach, dude. Don't call us if you get stranded.

I had a moment of panic, but I googled where we were and saw it was only a two-hour walk from my house. The knowledge was empowering. Whatever, I could walk. No problem.

It took some time to put myself back together—I splashed water on my face and gargled using some mouthwash I found— but eventually I was freshened up and ready to reenter the party, only to find it'd just ended.

Two people were making out on a couch in the living room, and the whole rest of the house was dark. I hung awkwardly around the couple—I sort of knew them—but their hands swarmed over each other, and they ignored me.

Then I heard a familiar voice. ". . . not worth it. . . ."

The lights were on upstairs. I walked gently on the carpeted steps, trying not to make a sound, and when I saw the cracked bedroom door, I said, "Hello? Umm, hello."

Nobody answered. So I crept closer. Avani was clearly ranting about Carrie.

". . . so disrespectful . . ."

"It's okay," Jessie said. "It's really okay."

Now my foot creaked on a patch of hardwood. I knocked twice on the door, then pushed it open. "He-hello."

A moment of silence, then a sudden scream.

"What?!" I said. "It's me!"

"Oh." Avani had ducked into a closet—I guess she wasn't wearing pants. "Fuck. It's okay. It's okay. It's Nandan," she said from behind the door.

"I was in the bathroom," I said. "And everyone left?"

Jessie covered her mouth with her hand and laughed. She was fully dressed, albeit in a pair of striped pajamas.

"Nandan, what're you doing?" Avani said. "Get out."

"I don't know. I just wanted to hang out."

"This is private!"

"It's about Carrie?" I said. "Sorry about that. . . ."

"Come on, Avani," Jessie said. "He's drunk. Just put on some of my sweats. It's Nandan."

I gave them a weak smile. "Yeah, it's me."

Jessie waited in the hall, smiling broadly.

"Thanks, Jessie," I said. "You're the good one. I always liked you."

"I know."

"You do?"

"Yeah, umm, you've said that to me, like, a bunch of times."

"How many?"

"Every time you get drunk, maybe? Yeah, around one a.m. on every night you get drunk."

"Well it's clearly true then!"

"Of course it is."

"Is Avani pissed about Carrie not coming?"

Jessie nodded.

"It's got to be hard," I said. "For you."

"No, it's okay. I don't care."

I had a complicated thought brewing in my head about how because Avani was so mad, that meant Jessie didn't have the room to be mad, because if Jessie got mad too, then Carrie would get kicked out of the group. It was hard to have to be the glue keeping those two together. But I couldn't quite put the whole thing into words.

"Avani said you and Hen are becoming friends," Jessie said.

"Yeah," I said. "He's amazing. I always thought he could never be serious, which meant it was exhausting to talk to him, but actually—"

The bedroom door opened. "How are you getting home?" Avani said.

"Walking?"

"Do you need to borrow a jacket or something?"

"I dunno. Maybe?"

"Avani!" Jessie said.

Jessie pulled me into her room. She sat on the bed, and Avani took a place on the window seat. The house was on the smallish side, and the roof above us was sloped, so I could only stand upright in the middle of the room, but I eventually took a seat at Jessie's desk, which put Avani and me as far as we could possibly be from each other.

"Umm, you won't vomit, will you?" Jessie said.

"Nope." I was about to add *not again* but stopped myself.

"Still, putting you in my parents' bed seems dangerous."

"I'll call him an Uber," Avani said.

My heart pounded. "I, uhh, I could stay here."

Avani's face instantly got very red and angry in a way I'd never seen before, but I cut in on her impending explosion. "I mean just to talk! You guys are worked up, and I could help strategize. I'm more of a Carrie type—no offense—I have insight—"

What I wanted was to be part of the sleepover. I wanted

87

so badly to stay in this room with the two of them and gossip about Carrie until our faces fell off, but I couldn't communicate that. The words didn't exist.

Jessie said, "I think our talk is gonna be a little intense. Anyway you should really go home and drink some water."

On the way home, I messaged Henry, and he answered immediately.

The whole story about wanting to stay and hang out with Avani and Jessie poured out of me instantly, without trouble, and he joked back:

> **Henry**: If they knew you were queer, you wouldn't have been able to get away.
>
> **Me**: Is the gay best friend still a thing?
>
> **Henry**: Believe me, it's still every straight girl's favorite fashion accessory.
>
> **Me**: What do you get out of it?
>
> **Henry**: Nothing, because I don't play that game. I hate when they _touch_ me. It makes my skin crawl.
>
> **Me**: To be honest, I think I'd like that.
>
> **Henry**: Well you're maybe not as fully gay as I am.
>
> **Henry**: I'm sorry, was I policing your sexuality? One of them—cough cough, it was Carrie—once got mad at me for policing her sexuality.
>
> **Me**: Yes, you were, to be honest. But I don't care. Dude,

you're the best. Thank you so much for being awake.

Henry: I'm always awake for my TSGB.

I asked what that meant, and he said it was his mental nick-name for me: the second gay boy.

Henry: I'm still the first, obviously. You need to kill me
and eat my heart to gain my powers.

Me: Or eat something else?

Henry: Nandan! That's so crass! We're not just all about
sex, you know.

I kept the conversation going for a few minutes after I got home, but eventually I fell asleep with my phone in my hand.

7

THE NEXT MORNING I APOLOGIZED to Pothan.

Me: The thing is, I actually liked the party. It was a little more chill than the beach would've been.
Pothan: You were just drunk and belligerent, dude. I get it. Don't worry.

That was the last weekend of the summer, and the beginning of school was a relief. By now the hangover had become permanent, and positive emotions were so far in the past that I could barely remember how they felt.

School wasn't actually too different from the summer: I lived to see the members of the Ninety-Nine coming together in various configurations, and I loved how school let me see everybody every day (without having to get trashed in order to do it). The only problem was that my classes were light on members of the Ninety-Nine, which meant my real life mostly consisted of the spaces between periods. This year Avani was in history with me, and Carrie was in my film criticism elective, but the real shock was heading into my last-period class, pre-calculus, and seeing Mari in the front row.

"Nandan!" she said. "I didn't know you were in this."

"Umm, you're the one who shouldn't be in this class."

"I know, but my dad made me take trig over the summer, so now I'm skipped ahead a year in math." She looked around. "I don't know anyone here."

I yawned. "Well you know me, and I know you."

Since the seats next to Mari were taken, I asked her to join me in the back row.

"Are you sure about this?" I said, as she picked up her back-pack. "Because where you sit today is where you'll sit for the rest of the year. And you seem like a front-row person."

"I am," she said. "But I can manage it. I just got new glasses, so . . ."

They were big, thick black frames that butted against her bangs.

"Keep them clean, or you'll get all blind like Dave," I said.

"I know!" she said. "Does he *ever* wash them? How do they get *so* bad?"

We chatted for a few minutes about Dave. They'd gone out again the day before, this time to another movie, and she grimaced when I asked how it'd gone.

"Come on," I said. "Dave won't tell me anything."

"How're you even friends with him?" she said.

"Just from around. He comes out. We talk."

"Oh my God." Her voice lurched abruptly into the split second of silence. "You guys were so embarrassing at the mall. I almost died when Henry said that stuff."

"But did it work?"

Now she looked at me shyly from over her hand. "Why do you care so much?" she said. "It's not bad! But you really do a lot for him."

I shrugged. "Just want to help, I guess."

"Well, we've been texting, but . . ." Her lips twitched. "I don't think he's actually into me."

"He's just shy."

"I know. It'll be fine." Her smile lifted her glasses and made huge dimples in her cheeks.

Then the teacher started talking about tests and expectations and homework, the way they tend to do, and I held my phone under the desk to text Dave.

Me: Hey what's going on with Mari?!

Me: You getting anxious again?

I had thought I was free after school, but Pothan texted me roughly thirty seconds after class ended.

Pothan: Yo, I'm outside. Jump in the car.

At that moment, my stomach issued a severe protest: *Noooooooooooo.*

Me: Umm, I have plans.
Pothan: What? Fuck you, what plans do you have?
Me: I shouldn't kiss and tell.
Pothan: Oh, bullshit. Who're you seeing? The alt girl from the beach?

I hid out in the library and crept home on foot, terrified that Pothan would burst out of nowhere and kidnap me again. When I finally got into my apartment, I put some water in the kettle and settled down for some television, texting, and tea.

I wrote Avani.

Me: Okay, this stays between us, right?
Avani: Sure! What's going on? My lips are sealed.

Her reply was instant, but I was wary. I wanted to talk about how Pothan was starting to bore me, but with Avani you never knew if something would get out or not, and if Pothan knew I'd blown him off just to hang out by myself, he might get angry enough to drop me. Or to turn cruel and mean like Lyle would've.

Me: Never mind.
Avani: K, hope you're all right.

Instead I texted Dave again.

Me: Okay how're you and Mari?
Me: WHAT IS GOING ON?!?!
Me: NEEEEEEEEEED ANSWERS
Me: She's wondering if you really like her. You could've come to me for advice you know.
Dave: Sorry, just been busy.
Me: Come on, what's happening between you two?

He didn't respond, and I already saw us texting nonsense back and forth, dodging each other's questions—our friendship slowly dying on the rocks of the forever-unsaid—and the idea made me so sad that I called him.

"Hey," he said. "I really don't have much time."

"Dave," I said. "You can talk to me."

"Can I?"

"What does that mean?"

"Nothing. I'm busy."

With Pothan or Ken, that would've been enough—I never would've brought up the subject again—but Dave was different. I wheedled with him, darting around the question *Are we okay?* in a dozen different ways, blatantly ignoring his attempts to get off the phone, exploiting all the tiniest little gaps and evasions in what he said, and, like a perp under the bright lights for ten hours, he finally broke.

"You know at the mall, I just wanted to hang out," he said. "But you guys acted really weird."

"Oh, shit," I said. "That's what this is about."

"I may not even like her," he said. "I don't *know*."

"Dude, giving each other a hard time is a key part of being friends. And, anyway, trying to get with a girl is never pretty, it's never not awkward."

Dave didn't say anything, but I heard him breathing over the phone, and my stomach twisted with the memory of his thighs under my hands.

"Hey," I said. "Is this about us hooking up?"

"What?" he said. "No."

"Because, like, we should've talked about it. That was your first time ever—"

"That was fine."

The heavy pounding of my heart made me hop off the couch and walk in narrow circles around the edges of the living room. I went to the door and listened with half my brain to see if my mom was home.

"You know, it doesn't mean anything about you. Come on, this isn't, like, the fifties: a straight guy can fool around," I said.

"No, no, I know. That's not a problem for me."

"I told Henry about it," I said. "Oh, shit, I told Henry. And I used your name. Shit. I outed—" I was about to say *outed you* but realized that wasn't quite right.

"That's fine."

"What? Really?"

"I don't care. I'm glad you're talking to someone." I heard the unspoken words: *someone who isn't me.*

"Wow, that's astonishingly cool. I think I'd be pissed if you'd gone telling people. Wait . . . you haven't . . . ?"

"No," he said. "But Henry is good. Obviously he's the one to tell. And you two are good friends."

"We're really not. But I guess we are now? Honestly I think he's just lonely."

"Hmm. Well . . . it's good he has you."

"You know I've sort of ghosted Hen, and it's awful. But if he and I keep talking all intense, then we'll end up together. Like, it *will* happen. And I don't know if I want that."

"But he's nice. You could do worse."

"Henry is *not* nice. That's what I like about him."

"Yeah, I guess you were with Avani, so . . ."

"What does that mean?!"

He laughed, and I heard the smile in his voice. "Well, she's not nice either. Maybe that's your thing."

"Wait, so now you're making fun of me?"

"You have a type. Like, you wouldn't go for a Mari."

"Why? Because she's nice and sweet and genuine? You gotta be kidding me. I love Mari. She's amazing. We're in math together. Did I tell you this?"

I let the conversation drift into gossip and talking about our day and all that other fun-but-irrelevant stuff. I kept pausing, waiting for Dave to say goodbye, but then he would leap in with some question or some joke, and we'd circle around again.

Then he said, "Hey . . . it's okay if you're not ready to be public. Henry would understand. You should talk to him."

"No, I know he'd keep it quiet. The real problem is . . . Okay . . . wait. . . . This is a real secret. Please do not tell anyone. Do I— Wait, you haven't agreed yet."

"I won't tell anyone."

"The real problem is I don't think I even like guys! It's just that sometimes I'm out with Pothan and Ken, and I'm like, *This is boring. I am boring.* And being gay seems like a big, shiny way of escaping it all. Isn't that pathetic?"

"Not if that's who you are."

"But it's not," I said. "Guys used to risk death to have sex with each other. That's not me. It's fine, but whatever. Not unmissable. The role, the title—that's what I want. But that'd be fake."

"Nandan . . . ," he said. "You should talk to someone."

"What? A guidance counselor? Dude, this is such a common

problem. Everybody wants to be queer these days. It's almost a cliché. Like, that's what stops me—it'd just be *sad*—can you imagine me standing up and being like, *Oh, I like guys?*—It'd be so pathetic—such attention whoring."

"It wouldn't be sad. It'd be honest."

"You know what I mean."

"I actually don't. Your real friends would get it."

Dave wouldn't get off the subject. He kept saying if I wanted to talk, he'd listen, and after a while it made me angry. Dave knew the truth. He'd been a weirdo since day one of high school, and nobody had ever applauded his "courage." With someone like Henry, it was different. He couldn't help being who he was. But with me—everyone would know it was a ploy for attention.

Which, to be fair, was exactly what it was!

The only way to escape was to be like Carrie. Stay mostly on the DL about the whole thing until you popped up and were like, *Hey, here's my girlfriend.* Then you weren't coming out. You weren't asking for anything. The whole queer thing was just a natural corollary of finding somebody you liked.

"Hey, and . . . if you ever want . . . ," Dave said, "me to, uhh"—his voice dropped to a whisper—"come over . . . I still, uhh, I still owe you for the other night. And maybe you want to practice for Hen, or, uhh, just figure things out."

"Dave," I said. "Whoa, are you making a move?"

"I guess?"

"That's so direct! I'm proud of you. I mean maybe a little more subtlety with Mari. Girls like that. But for someone like me, it'd be perfect."

"Oh, thanks."

"All right, I gotta go."

A few minutes after I signed off, he texted me, asking if that was a no on his coming over and hanging out. And I suddenly had this vision of him sitting in his room, sweaty and anxious, tapping out a reply.

Me: No, man, I don't think I want to hook up again. It'd just be weird. You're a friend now!

I was gonna write more, about how anyway he wasn't really gay, he was just horny and eager to please, but I deleted that part, because that wasn't for me to judge. Still, I didn't think Dave was serious about any of this. He just wanted to mess around. That was his first sexual experience ever! It must've been so confusing. If your first time ever getting a blow job was from a guy friend, it'd really have you wondering about yourself.

My conversation with Dave must've done some good, because a few days later I came into math, and Mari was literally bouncing up and down in her back-row seat.

"Hey," I said. "What's going—"

"Dave and I talked again last night." Her eyes were aglow. "He called me!"

"Awesome," I said. "That's so cool."

Now her hand touched my arm. "Did you have something to do with that?"

I looked down at her unpainted nails. "What do you mean?"

"Come on. You gave him a pep talk or something."

"Nope. It's all him. I realized my help wasn't really helping. He needed to do things on his own."

"Well, it was great. He was so different! But totally the same! Dave's really amazing."

Someone sat directly in front of us, and Mari's voice quieted, but I could still feel the excitement. He had picked her up in his car, and they'd just driven up to Shoreline. I got the impression, though she didn't say it, that they'd made out a bit, and maybe done a bit more. I followed her out of class afterward, wanting to know the details, and she just winked at me and said, "We'll talk later, okay?"

I was about to be like, *Err, okay, except you don't have my number*, but she was already hurrying in the direction of her next class.

8

LATER THAT WEEK I GOT a text from Dave himself.

Dave: Hey so you know Mari's been asking if we can hang out with you and Avani and Hen again?

Me: I was aware. We are an incredible trio. A team of Avengers, you might say.

Dave: Well she heard about the lake house, and I guess she's asking if we can see it.

Me: Whoa, what? Are you kidding? People don't _ask_ to see the lake house.

Dave: I didn't know. Okay, I'll tell her it's not doable.

Me: What is this about? Dude, that makes her sound like she only wants to climb the social ladder. Which is not who I thought she was at all.

Dave: Don't worry about it, seriously. And don't mention this to Mari okay? I'll talk to her. I don't want things to be awkward.

But the conversation actually made me a little mad. I'd never considered that by showing up on his date, we'd made Dave seem like a bigger deal. Hanging out with a guy just because he was cool or popular was sleazy, but it was normal. Usually you don't even *know* if you like them or if you just like their place in the world—everything is so inextricably and deliciously intermingled that by the time you figure it out, the fling is over. But Dave hadn't signed up for that treatment, and he'd be crushed if Mari turned out not to be interested in the real Dave.

When Avani texted me a few days later to ask why Dave was asking about the lake house, I couldn't think of anything to say except the truth.

We both agreed this wasn't right and that somebody needed to question Mari about what was happening. Avani sometimes isn't the most gentle person in the universe, so I said I'd talk to Mari the next day during our last-period class together.

But before I saw her, I spotted Dave, all alone at a faraway picnic table, looking so pale and worn-out that I wondered if Mari had already dropped him. As I crossed the grass, he got larger and larger in my vision, but he didn't wave or smile, just sat with his head propped in his arms, staring dully into the distance.

"Hey," I said.

"Oh." The corners of his lips twitched, then turned lifeless again. "What's up?"

"What're you doing out here? Pondering the meaning of life?"

"Sort of."

I took a seat across from him, and he drew back, retracting like a worm, until he was in a more upright position.

"I heard you talked to Avani about the lake house. I bet that didn't go well."

He grimaced. "It was pretty awkward."

"Did Mari handle it okay?"

"Yeah, okay, so . . . I think you got the wrong idea about that." He scanned to make sure nobody was close. "Mari didn't really *ask* to see the lake house. She just got *interested* in it, and I wanted to impress her by inviting her there."

"You don't need to do that."

"I know. I guess."

"Because it can be a turnoff if somebody tries too hard."

"Except—" His eyes rose toward mine. "I kinda just want to make her happy."

"Well, I'm sorry, bro. Maybe some other time. But I guess shit's going pretty well between you?"

"I don't know. I mean . . ." He took a breath. "We've already hooked up, so that's out of the way, but I don't know what's next."

The air blew out of my chest and straight through my nose, splattering him with a misting of snot. "What? You've hooked up?"

"I mean, yeah, little stuff. But it was good. And I think she likes me, but I don't know. It's so weird and awkward. I just want it to be normal. I mean." He shook his head. "I really like her. I really, really like her."

"Dude," I said. "That's fantastic. That's incredible. You're totally golden."

"I guess. But I kind of wish we could, like, get this part over with? Like, I don't know: have sex, be, like, *You're my boyfriend; sounds good, let's go to homecoming together*, and stuff like that. Instead of this incredible paralyzing awkwardness, every day, all the time." He shook his head. "I don't know. Maybe I should just talk to her—ask, like, *What do you want?* Or should I be bolder? Say I want more?"

"Dude! Dude! Don't rush things. You're in a great place." I leaned forward, my fingertips just an inch from his. "You know what? I'm gonna tell you a secret now, Dave. This is a real secret.

"Okay? You ready?" I said. "Sex isn't that great. I mean it's okay. It feels good, but is it an order of magnitude better than masturbating? Mmmmmmm . . . not really. In some ways it's worse. No . . . what's good is being with someone. Touching them. Looking into their eyes. Shit like that. Shit you have. I envy you, Dave. I envy you. I've never had that. With me it's always been parties at the beach, alcohol, hanging over some girl, wondering whether at the end of the night you both'll be drunk enough to—"

I coughed, then my voice got a little louder. "Dude, you are so great. You're so honest. You're so kind. You have exactly the thing that most girls search for inside a Pothan or a Ken and *never* manage to find."

He blinked, and I thought I had him. But then he gave me a sigh and pulled away. I could feel the understanding deplete like the stamina meter in a video game.

The thing is, I knew exactly what was going through his head. He just wanted to be loved. Or not even that. Actually that's the crazy thing—it's hard to *feel* loved. What really feels good is when somebody else is willing to accept your love. He was walking around with all this love in his pockets and nobody to spend it on.

"You really like her that much?" I said. "You're sure about her?"

He nodded.

"Okay . . . the thing is . . . normally I wouldn't let you do something like this. The weird thing about people is that the more somebody loves us, the more we pull away from them. And doing something like this—taking her to the lake house— it's sort of, like, it could backfire."

For a brief moment his face scrunched up and got dark, and

I got a glimpse of a harder side to Dave: the guy who'd waited in the corners, never speaking, at so many different parties.

"But, but, but hold on," I said. "If she's the right person, she'll love it. And Dave . . . you don't deserve anything less than the right person."

"Yeah." He gulped. "So . . . what?"

"Let's do it. Let's get ourselves invited to the lake house."

"You can do that? I thought Avani wasn't into it."

"For you, bro, I can make it happen."

9

"HELLO?"

Avani sounded surprised to get my call. I was at the breakfast table, perched on the edge of the seat with my back straight, as if this was a real serious business call about some real serious business, but she couldn't see that, and I tried to project a tone that suggested I was bored and lying on a couch somewhere.

"Talk to me," I said.

"Err . . . what's happening right now?"

"I'm calling you."

"But . . . why?"

"Just to see how you're doing."

I'd realized that if I mentioned the lake house, Avani would shut me down, so I needed an indirect approach.

"Uhh, I'm fine," she said.

"Well, it just occurred to me," I said, "that nobody's seen you out in, like, three or four weeks at least."

"In two weeks."

"So it's a thing. The old Avani never would've disappeared for two weeks."

"Just haven't been feeling it."

I wanted to keep pushing her, but while I was thinking of what to say, her voice rushed into the silence, and she said, "At least when you and me were hanging out, I could look forward to that."

Now I realized the power of silence. Instead of saying something, I made a noise in the back of my throat, and the words spilled out of her.

"It's not as if you were that great. But you were sort of in the right ballpark. Now it's just Pothan and Ken. And Carrie's learning from them."

Another noise from my throat.

"Nobody needs or wants me. Last year I was only a sophomore, and all I needed was to perform like a monkey, and it was fun, because I was so young. This year, I need to *be* somebody, and I'm just not."

My silence went on for a long time. Avani had never been this honest with me before. I wanted to jump in and say, *I feel exactly the same!*, but I didn't.

"You and me should've gotten together for real," she said.

"We'd have been a unit. Now it's too late. I don't know; it doesn't matter. This is all so *stupid*. My sister says I won't care about any of this stuff after high school ends."

Again I said nothing. Some mysterious force pulled me back, snuffed out my personality, and let Avani just explore her own thoughts as if I wasn't even around.

"The thing is," she said, "on the beach I'm basically nobody. The things you and I are good at—the talking—it doesn't matter there. But . . . do you remember the lake house?"

"Mmm-hmmm?"

"Well, my parents have been asking what weekend I want to invite my friends over. Jessie and Carrie and I have done this for, like, years, but Carrie already said she won't go if her girlfriend, Gabriela, can't come, and I was like, 'Fuck you, then let's not do it.'"

"That sucks. You used to have all these plans about maybe using the lake house more this year."

"Yeah . . . I guess. . . . But you know I'd never throw a party. That's the dumbest thing on earth. People who throw parties are so desperate. Nobody respects them."

This was dangerous ground. Avani on some level really wanted to have people over. She wanted to host and to feel important. But last year whenever somebody threw a party, Lyle would lead the entire Ninety-Nine in the task of completely trashing their house.

"You're right. You could never have something big there."

"I could never have anything. You know how out of control things get."

"Totally. It's best to not use it."

Now I waited, my heart beating fast.

"Still, something small might be cool," she said.

"You'd need the right people, or it would totally degenerate," I said.

"Yeah. How many, though?"

Again, my tongue swerved to the side and avoided making a suggestion: "Actually, just the three of you was probably the best number."

"But with Gabriela along too it'd be so awkward."

"Then maybe . . ." I smiled, because now my brain had caught up with my tongue, and I realized my strategy. "Maybe twenty people?"

"Way too crazy," she said. "But I don't know? Eight or nine?"

"You sure it wouldn't get too crazy?"

"No, I don't think so. Not if they were the right people."

"I guess. And the nice thing is, it's not like you're letting Gabriela invade your totally private thing that you used to do with Carrie and Jessie. Instead, you're killing the old thing and creating something new for her."

"Exactly!"

I heard a rustling on the other end of the phone. "But who should come?"

At this point I was about to say *me*, but I stopped myself, and I let that force flow through me again. "Who do you think?"

"I don't know. I was thinking Henry. You two are close. You could ask him, right?"

"Uhh."

"Come on," Avani said. "What, are you insecure about spending the weekend with a gay guy?"

Avani was living in a glass house. I wanted to deliver a jab about how she was desperate to have a gay best friend, but that'd probably destroy everything.

"Sure. I can ask Henry."

Now was the trickiest part. If Avani got any hint that this thing wasn't entirely about *her*, she would back out. And if I mentioned Dave at all, she'd put two and two together and be, like, wait a second, are you doing this for *him*? Dave's name was stuck in my throat: I knew that mentioning him would blow up this entire plan, but I needed to get him invited.

She rumbled on. "But it's only two guys: you and Hen. Seems lopsided. Do you think I should invite Pothan and Ken?"

"Uhh . . ."

"They're a lot of fun."

"You already have Carrie there. She's gonna try to make things wild."

"Well it's not gonna be like when we were twelve and my mom was upstairs. It's gonna be a little wild, probably."

"I . . . if that's what you want."

"And I don't want them to feel left out."

"Yeah . . . yeah. Okay. Let's do it."

She had a few more doubts and insecurities, and I talked her through it, but all the while I marveled at my own power. This was magical. It really was. After a solid year of trying to talk her into inviting me, all it'd taken was to let her talk *herself* into it. Now all I needed was to somehow get Dave onto the guest list.

At lunch a few days later, Carrie plopped down on a bench next to me.

"Welcome to hell," she said.

"Uhh, hey."

"What're you eating?"

I shrugged. "It's pizza day."

"Gross."

She unwrapped a protein bar and picked off a little end of it for me.

"Umm, thanks."

I was at a table in the corner of one of the courtyards, trying to do some last-minute studying for a chem exam, while rain poured, just a few feet away, over the lip of the overhang and down into the muddy strip of grass between the buildings.

"Avani has reached seventy-five percent lake-house insanity," Carrie said. "She sent me a *packing* list for Gabriela, to make sure she's 'fully able to participate.'"

"Wow." I sat silent for a few moments. "But . . . that's kind of good, ri—"

"No, it's not good. This weekend will be a nightmare of unparalleled proportions."

"I disagree. How is it gonna be bad?"

"Not sure," Carrie said. "I'm really not sure. But she's making us all drive together in one car, and you know it's twenty miles away, right? We're going to be *trapped* there together, totally subject to all her drama."

Carrie slumped down like a deactivated robot, but I was smiling. She began a story about last year, when Avani had completely freaked out because Carrie had to leave a few hours early.

"Okay, okay, okay, but . . . it's 'cause she's worried about losing you."

I tried to press things further, telling Carrie that if she'd just reassure Avani that they were still good friends, then things would be better, but Carrie cut me off and started asking about my homecoming plans.

"This makes me think Avani will try to corral us into it again," Carrie said. "And I'm thinking I should just swoop in and plan something first."

"What? Last year was fun."

"Uhh, was it? If we hadn't bought into her homecoming plans, she wouldn't have been able to deliver us up like little bunny rabbits to Lyle Brashear's horrible party."

We had all intended to go to homecoming together: me and Avani, Ken and Jessie, and Carrie (sort of) with Pothan. But at the last minute, as we were literally on the way to the dance, Pothan got a text saying they were locking people in, not letting them leave, and he simultaneously got all these pictures from Lyle Brashear's immense bacchanalian anti-homecoming party.

Pothan and Avani huddled together in the back of the limo for a few minutes, debating things, before agreeing to redirect the driver to Lyle's place instead.

"So you didn't love Lyle's?" I said.

"I liked that homecoming dress. And if I'd known I was only getting dressed up so I could stand around watching Lyle play drinking games, I'd have just stayed home. Anyway, maybe this year I'll do my own thing."

"I can't imagine what kind of party you'd plan," I said. "It'd be insane."

She hit me on the shoulder. "I'm not insane all the time. It'd be nice! But maybe we could do something a little more exciting: go to a show or something."

Then she got a call, and she said, "Yeah, yeah, I'm over between buildings eleven and twelve," and a guy and a girl, members of the Ninety-Nine, swooped in with a bag of sandwiches.

They nodded hi to me, and I nodded to them, and we ate together quite happily while they talked about some band they all wanted to see.

Over the next two weeks, Avani reached what Carrie would probably call 100 percent lake-house craziness. Jessie and Carrie bore the brunt of it. She wanted them to come a day early—Gabriela wasn't allowed, obviously—to help make decorations. She wanted to plan their outfits for each day. She wanted each person to take charge of one meal.

I thought it was delightful, and I tried to convince them that this was real friendship. She did this stuff because she loved them. I also texted Avani a few times and asked if she needed any help, but each time she was like, "Thanks! I'll tell you if I think of anything."

Meanwhile I'd told Dave to invite Mari, and although I knew it'd work out, my stomach was in knots, worried that Mari would try to talk to Avani. In a world where people get murdered or starve to death every day, this was a pretty minor problem, but I couldn't sleep for thinking every night, *How am I going to do this?* My mind went around in circles, first saying, *Well, worst comes to worst I'll just show up with them,* then saying, *Oh, shit, but that'll ruin everything,* and then saying, *Well, whatever, is Avani going to get mad and send everybody home?*

Then of course there was Henry. I had held off on asking him to the lake house, hoping Avani would forget, because I felt awkward about the two of us. He and I still texted on occasion, but nothing like those long, intense conversations we used to have.

Part of me wondered whether this lake-house visit might not be an opportunity. If I invited Hen, we could share a room, get drunk, and, I don't know, explore the idea of being something to each other. A practice boyfriend, at least. Or maybe a real one. If I was gonna come out, doing it with a dude already in tow would be best. And Hen seemed game for it. But despite these thoughts I somehow couldn't manage to actually *send* the text.

When Avani brought him up again, I said maybe she ought to make the call, because he and I weren't really close anymore. But she said, "If I ask, he won't come."

"Why not?" I said. "He likes you."

"I don't think so."

"Of course he does."

It turned out she was right. When I ducked into his homeroom and asked him to the lake house, he was really cagey, asking who else would be there, and when I told him the guest list, he said, "Okay, well I like Carrie, and you're great, obviously, but I don't know Jessie that well."

I threw my head back. "Come on, it'll be a caper!"

A group of kids filed past to get into the room, and we drifted down the path. "You can't keep convincing me by saying 'It's a caper.' That only works once."

"Look, all right. The truth is . . ." I took a breath and told him about Dave and Mari. I thought I'd made the situation sound sweet, but Hen didn't seem to care.

"You know . . . all this effort over Dave, but he likes girls. He can hook up with anybody. I'm the person who needs help, but nobody's ever like, *Oh, let's set up Hen.*"

"Well, then let's do that. Who're your prospects?"

"No, it has to be natural. This is not . . ." He shook his head. "Look, I'm a little tired of being a guest star on the Avani Show."

"This isn't that. It's the Nandan Show."

"She's okay, and I get why *you* would like her." At my expression, he said, "She's hot. I'm saying she's hot, and you like girls, and you think with your dick, obviously."

"Yeahhhh . . . that's true. But there's more to it than that. Pleeeease. Come on."

A bell sounded, and Hen had to get back to class. He hadn't agreed, but I still went away excited. These conversations were the ones I wanted to be having. Light and fun, without sacrificing depth. I could've gone to a dozen T99 parties with Hen and never learned that he didn't like Avani or that he felt bad about his (lack of a) love life.

When I told that to Mari before precalc, she said, "But if you want to know that stuff, just ask."

"You can't just ask. There has to be a moment."

"It sounds like Hen's lonely," she said. "I know how that is. Before I started making an effort to make more friends, I got lonely all the time."

Her serious tone made her seem really young. She didn't know Hen that well. He was one of the best-liked people in our class. Everybody thought he was amazing. If he was lonely, it was because he didn't let people get close.

"But not anymore?" I said.

"Well, now I have you! And Dave!"

"You two really seem to get along."

"Yeah, ever since I stopped expecting anything from him."

"Mari . . . Dave is really into you."

"I don't think so."

"He did all this for you, Mari. Set up the lake house and everything, because *you* wanted it."

"Umm, well, okay. That's really nice."

I gritted my teeth. Part of me wanted to be stern and be like, *What the hell, Mari, you shouldn't be like this. Why are you pulling away from Dave already?* Except I knew it wouldn't have helped.

But now I had a new problem. I wasn't even sure this party was going to *work*. Dave had fallen into exactly the trap I'd expected—he'd tried too hard and scared her away.

That night, willing to say and do whatever it took, I messaged Hen.

Me: Hey, dude.

Henry: Hey.

Me: I'm sorry I've been weird.

Me: Questioning my sexuality was a little exhausting.

Henry: Lol, no worries.

Me: I still have no idea if I'm queer.

Me: Sometimes I wonder if I'm just in love with the idea of it.

Me: Other times I'm like, yeah okay I want to have sex with guys.

Me: Honestly, I feel really protective toward Dave. Part of why we hooked up is I wanted him to feel good about himself. That was his first anything ever.

Henry: I hope he appreciated it.

Me: He did.

Me: I don't know. The thing between him and me is so weird. I look at him, and it's like my heart is getting pulled out of my chest. I just want to protect him. We've known each other for a while, and he's never quite gotten there, never quite found his place.

Me: Part of me thinks he's what I could've been. If Avani hadn't picked me. If Pothan hadn't brofriended me. If I hadn't learned I was worth something.

Henry: You two are pretty different. Dave just seems shy and quiet.

Me: I feel bad. His thing with Mari is falling apart. He really likes her. It's crazy. Like love-love. And he's so close. That's the worst, when you're almost there, but for some reason, they won't quite see you that way.

Me: I want this to happen for him, but I need your help. Avani won't invite him if I ask, but she will for you.

Henry: I don't get it. All this angst over Dave.

Henry: But I'll do it.

Henry: You owe me now! Someday I'll ask you for

119

something, and if you refuse, well, there'll be no real punishment. But you better not refuse!

Me: I won't.

My heart beat faster. Even though it'd be incredibly sleazy, and Hen wasn't that kind of person, part of me thought he might want me to, err, do things to him. And I wasn't certain I'd say no.

Henry: All right then, I suppose we're on for another caper.

10

ON THE DAY OF THE party, Pothan showed up at my apartment wearing one of his absurd getups: a white vest on a white shirt, wool pants, and lizard-skin shoes topped with white spats.

He threw himself into our love seat. "Ken's gonna drive separate. He's got practice today."

"Uhh . . . sure."

Pothan slumped down on the couch and spread his legs, as if his junk was so heavy it needed to rest directly on the cushion.

"Okay if I just leave my stuff outside?" Pothan said. "Or we gonna be here for a while?"

He hopped to his feet and paced the room. This was his pre-party "getting worked up" routine. He stretched his arms a few times, then smiled and relaxed his face and smiled again.

"So we're here to get Dave laid? That's the plan?" Avani was so happy that Hen had accepted the party invite that she hadn't batted an eye when I told her Dave and Mari were coming too.

"No, I'm just gonna nudge things in the right direction. It's really not your problem."

"Dude, of course it's my problem. The bro of my bro is my bro. That's, like, that's science. That's genetics, bro."

"Not necessarily, I mean if Dave and I were stepbrothers and you and I were stepbrothers, then you might not even *know* Dave and—"

"I didn't say stepbro or half bro or bro-in-law. I said bro."

"That's a good point, actually."

"So what's the game plan? Carrie's a lesbian now, and I guess her girlfriend is too. Dave's bringing his girl. Avani's yours. So probably Ken and me and Hen'll be having a threesome." His eyes glinted.

"Avani isn't mine. She is so far from mine. And you forgot Jessie!"

"Oh yeah! So now the numbers really work. Ken and I arm-wrestle. Winner gets Hen and loser gets Jessie."

I rolled my eyes.

"Hen is *hot*." Pothan made a fist like he was gripping a hard cock. "If I swung that way, he's the branch I'd swing from."

"It's true. And he's looking for somebody. Maybe you—"

Pothan barked a laugh. "That'd be so great. Can you imagine? No drama. My cousin is gay, and he says it's, like, sex always, all the time, everywhere, with strangers, people you

122

meet on apps, in clubs, on the street; you just lock eyes and get right down to fucking."

"Yeah . . . I don't know if that's been Hen's experience."

Dave rolled up a few minutes later, and we ran through the rain to his car. We picked up Hen around the corner from his house. He had just a backpack, and he gave us an automatic eye roll as he climbed in next to Pothan in the back.

"Are you absolutely sure we won't make it home tonight? If I don't come home, I do have an excuse prepared, but it's bound to be flimsy—I'm an awful liar—my parents always just think I'm telling a joke."

"I don't know . . . the lake house is pretty far," I said.

To be honest, Avani hadn't exactly said the guys would spend the night, though I knew when she and Jessie and Carrie hung out, they always did. But I was just gonna assume we would too.

Hen offered his hand, palm down, to Pothan, who took it and, swiftly, impulsively, kissed the back of his hand.

"Delighted to make your acquaintance," Pothan said.

Hen cackled. "You're my Prince Charming." I felt an odd stab of anger and jealousy. Incredibly, Pothan even had me beat when it came to homoerotic bonding. My eyes met Hen's, and he smiled back without a hint of awkwardness. All night I'd wrestled with the question of whether to start something with Hen tonight. Pothan's presence made it hard. And once we added Ken to the mix, the awkwardness would immediately kill any possible romance. But maybe tonight I could sneak him down to the lakeside and see where things went.

Pothan immediately took charge, telling Dave to stop at a gas station where he knew the owner. After he'd bought beer, he told us to carry it back to the car while he wandered over to the strip mall across the street, which sold high-tech racing bikes.

After fifteen minutes we tried to drag him out, but he got into a conversation with the heavily tattooed guy who was demoing the bikes, and Pothan made Dave surrender his car keys to the guy as collateral so we could ride the bikes around the parking lot.

Then of course we needed coffee, and Pothan was now totally charming again. The café was empty because it was morning and a weekend and this was an isolated patch of nowhere next to the freeway. Pothan spent ten minutes talking to the twenty-year-old barista, making jokes with her about foam latte art, while I cringed at his flirting.

Hen and Dave and I sat together at a table, and I could tell Pothan had entranced Hen. When his name got called for the coffee, Hen thanked the barista, who was pretty cute—she was Latina and wore hipsterish cat-eyed glasses—and asked if Pothan wasn't bothering her, and she giggled and said, "You guys are adorable," and of course she was only humoring the two of them, because obviously we're all high school kids, but it was so fun and so nice, and I sighed, because I hated my personality so much.

People liked me, and some perhaps even loved me, but I didn't *imprint* myself on people the way that a truly big personality does. I was nowhere near as beautiful and distinct and fearless as a Pothan or an Avani (or even a Carrie or a Hen). Right now I could either join Pothan at the counter, and look like a latecomer, or stay behind. And the thing was, a really dominant personality, somebody like Pothan, would just change the rules and maneuver things so that they looked good. Of course that was an asshole move, because it sucked out all the oxygen and left no place for anybody else, but it also worked, and it was *fun*. Hanging out here in the middle of nowhere was *fun*. If it'd just been me, this drive would've been completely boring, but he turned the journey itself into fun, and for the first time I was happy that he was coming along with us, since it helped me avoid the dreaded question: *What will we do once we're all up there?*

Because for better or worse, you never had a dull party with Pothan around.

The road up in the mountains, Route 17, was traffic-free, but it was also narrow and wet, and Dave dug his fingers into the wheel and stared directly forward, hands at ten and two o'clock like in a driving test, while the rest of us chattered around him.

Pothan looked up from his phone: "The girls got there like three hours ago."

"I hope Mari is okay," I said. "She's the odd one out."

"No, Carrie's girlfriend is the odd one out," Henry said. "I do not envy her. I think she might not live through this night. That's a major possibility."

"Avani should just go gay," Pothan said. "Carrie would be into that."

Nobody laughed, and I sensed Pothan, who's better than Ken at reading his audience, dialing back the gay jokes.

I'd gotten Mari's number in the run-up to planning this thing, and now I texted her.

Me: We're wondering how you're doing.

The response came back instantly.

Mari: Good! Just unpacking.
Me: Not too weird? Avani treating you okay?
Mari: If by that you mean "is she telling me what to do?" Then yes. I'd be annoyed, but everybody else is getting it way worse.
Mari: It's cool, though. I heard you're the one who got me invited (but it's a secret?). Thanks! Man, you and Avani and Pothan and Dave's friend stuff is so complicated.

At that I looked up and shot a glare at Dave. "Dude," I said. "Hmm?"

"You told Mari that I set this up?

"No . . . ," he said.

"She just told me you did."

"Oh," he said. "Yeah. I guess I must've."

We drove in silence until Pothan got restless: the upholstery creaked as he pressed his knees against the back of my seat and pushed outward.

"So you and your girlfriend are gonna fuck tonight?" Pothan said.

"Umm . . . ," I said. "It's not like that."

"I'm talking to the kid! Let me, let me, let me just talk, okay?"

Hen laughed. "You sound like Nandan now."

"Oh my God, yeah. The repeating words: 'And, and, and, and, and now I've got a pearl of wisdom for you.'"

The car laughed, and my face went red. Dave's voice broke through. "I don't think so. But it's not really a big deal."

"Oh, bullshit," Pothan said. "Of course it's a big deal. I'm not trying to give you a hard time. I'm just wondering if you need, like, some advice on how to close."

Dave's eyes were fixed on the road. The car went fast around a heart-stopping turn, and my hand shot out to support me, but Pothan, wedged in, stayed cool and motionless.

"What kind of advice?" Dave said.

"Take your pick." Pothan said. "I'm a full-service bro. First of all—" He reached into his pocket and pulled out a string of three condoms. Then he leaned forward and groped around on

Dave's chest before sliding the condoms into his shirt pocket. "Stay safe. You're too young to be a daddy."

This was only the beginning, and I was already tired of Pothan's performance, but Hen laughed, and his hand waved like a conductor's as he provided the transition line:

"And second of all?" Hen said.

"Wellllllllll," Pothan said. "The major thing is that girls want you to take charge. So it's this totally weird thing where neither of you explicitly talks about what's going to happen. For instance, you almost always have to find a BS reason to maneuver her into someplace you can be alone."

"I, uhh, we're alone in my car all the time," Dave said.

"Okay, okay, but there's the problem, because you don't know. Maybe she'll be like, 'Hey I need a ride home,' and you're like, 'Oh, wink wink, a ride home,' but it turns out she actually wants a ride home, and she feels really weird when you try something, and she just does it because shit's so awkward. No. Bad move. Better if it is something where she can meet you halfway, like if she says, 'Hey, I'm gonna crash here tonight,' and you're like, 'Oh, let's scope out the bedrooms. You know, just to check.' And you get up, and, you're like, 'This bed looks soft and shit. Let's test it out.' That way she can always be like, 'Err, no, why would I need you for that?' Or if she's not into it, you can leave, no problem. Because once you're on the bed you think it'd be simple, but, oh no, it doesn't stop being a game. Because then you've gotta be like, 'Oh, how's the party,' and you creep closer. And she's like, 'It was cool,' and she gets a little closer, and then you're snuggling on the bed, and at some point you're touching her all along her sides, all along her hips, then you're kissing, right? But are we being honest yet? No. Uh-uh, because now you've gotta start taking off clothes, but you gotta be careful, because maybe she doesn't want that now, so you go back to grinding on each other, but . . . after you do that . . . maybe she gets hot and changes her mind, but how do you know? You gotta try again, because she won't do anything—"

"Pothan," I said. "You're gonna scare him. It does not need to be like that."

"I don't know," Pothan said. "Just giving my experience."

Hen put up his hands. "Hey, it's all a mystery to me."

"Relax," I said. "If she wants it to happen, it will."

"No," Pothan said. "That is not correct advice. No girl wants to make a move. That's the basics. I'm not saying do anything creepy, but you need to make moves."

Now Dave's voice creaked into life. "Thanks. That all seems okay, but, like, I don't know if that'll happen tonight."

"All right . . . ," Pothan said. "But there's a second part. You make sure she enjoys it, you know"—then he launched into this description of how to touch her down there, how to be gentle, how to find the right spots . . .

"Where did you learn this stuff?"

"The internet, obviously."

Dave said, "I, uhh, heard some girls prefer anal. Like,

because it's not technically—"

"I don't know those girls," Pothan said. "That's a rumor, but seriously. I don't know anything about anal. You should ask Hen."

Again, Henry shrugged. "I dunno."

"What?" Pothan said. "You serious?

"Pothan . . . ," I warned.

"The truth is . . . that, uhh, at, uhh," Hen stammered, "at the parties we go to, there aren't really other guys who are into guys."

Dave and I exchanged a look. Pothan clapped Henry on the shoulder, and he was like, "That is fucking sad. Look, dude, we're gonna fix this."

Pothan asked Henry all kinds of questions, and as the strategizing continued, Hen started sitting sideways, leaning against the door, and began making fun of Pothan's outfit, which I knew meant he was feeling comfortable. I leaned against the window, not doing anything, just smiling to myself, as we came over the rise and saw the clear blue lake opening up beneath us.

11

SIX HOURS LATER, AVANI WAS puking upstairs while Jessie hovered over her; Hen was passed out on a nearby couch; and Ken, Pothan, and Carrie were on the back porch trying to build a homemade catapult out of some resistance bands and a pair of lacrosse sticks while Gabriela alternated between egging them on and trying to make them stop.

I sat in the living room with a dazed Mari and Dave. Half-drunk cans of beer were all over the kitchen table. At least two of those were mine. I'd opened each one absentmindedly, and both times Mari had given me a sharp look and said, "Hey, can you not get drunk right now?"

"Well," I said. "This . . . was not what I was expecting."

Mari had a tight-lipped smile. Dave lay back on the couch. He at least was sipping a beer.

"Really?" Dave said. "This is a surprise to you?"

"I don't know." I waved my hands. "It just . . ."

Things had been awkward from the beginning. We'd all stood around in the living room, staring at each other, trying to plan what to do. Avani suggested going down to the lake. At that moment Pothan opened a beer and challenged us to play king cup. Halfway through the game Carrie jacked up the music. The screaming and shouting began. Avani drank quickly, with a fixed look in her eyes, and finally staggered off with Jessie in tow. Hen at least seemed to be having fun. He kept punching Pothan and Ken and me in the sides, saying, "You guys . . . you guys . . ." And within two hours he and Pothan had developed a series of catchphrases that continued even now.

"Spur and ride!" Pothan whooped outside. "Spur and motherfucking ride!"

"The hay is in the barn!" Carrie shouted.

The nonsensical phrases seemed to have bubbled up from the formless noise that surrounded us while we drank.

My lips twitched. "Well, umm . . . ," I said. "I don't know if you guys want to sleep?"

"It's early," Mari said.

Dave's eyes were half closed. I poked him in the gut. "Uhh, yeah, it's early," he said.

Avani stumbled downstairs. Her face was pale and withered, and her hair was in wet strands across her back. The dress she'd arrived in was gone, replaced by sweatpants and a white

T-shirt. She opened one of the beers on the table and sniffed it, and a spasm ran across her stomach.

"Hey," I said. "You okay?"

"This is a nightmare," she said.

The venom in her voice stung Dave and Mari, sending them upright.

"Come on," I said. "It'll calm down soon—"

"I didn't even want to do this."

She went on, her voice rising, getting more frantic and emotional. Carrie looked in, raised an eyebrow, and dipped away. Avani got up, taking her just-opened can of beer to the sink. She poured it out, then went around, collected more cans, and carried each one to the sink.

"Umm, hey," Mari said. "Avani, let's talk."

Jess came downstairs, and she and Mari and Avani huddled in the kitchen. Dave took off his glasses, cleaned them, and put them on again. "What is happening?"

"They're smoothing down Avani's feathers."

"No, there's something more."

Checking to make sure Avani wasn't looking, I grabbed Dave around the head and brought him close, then kissed the top of his head. His body was hot and clammy under my hands.

"Thank God you're here," I said. "Seriously, what the fuck?"

"I am fascinated," Dave said. "This is, sociologically, very interesting."

"Is that why you put up with us? I mean you've been coming out for years, but you're always so quiet."

"No," he said. "I came to get laid."

I snorted.

"Seriously." His dark eyes transfixed me. "I couldn't make it happen, but that's why I came. It wasn't so bad. I mean, to be honest, I liked when things got crazy, and everyone got wrapped up in themselves, and I could just watch."

"Yeah. . . ."

"I mean look . . ."

Our eyes panned across the room. Pothan had come inside, and now he was flicking Hen on the face, trying to get him awake. Ken and Carrie were doing something in the back involving fire. Avani and Mari and Jessie were still muttering to themselves in the kitchen. We looked at all the figures, their words drowned out by the noise, and their movements made herky-jerky by the alcohol and bright lights.

"Yeah . . . ," I said. "It's nice."

Then Avani ran upstairs, and the girls followed her. When Avani reappeared: her face was wiped clean of makeup. She looked really young and really tired. Now she stumbled a bit, trying to put on her heels, and Jessie gave her a hand.

"Let me, umm, let me just talk to Carrie," Jessie said.

"Don't bother."

But Jessie opened the sliding door, and we heard the roar of voices and the blast of music from a portable speaker.

134

"Come on," Ken said. "What's wrong? What's wrong?"

"Nothing," Avani said. "I'm sick, and I'm going home. You can stay. It's fine."

"Okay," Carrie yelled. "See you later."

Outside, we saw Gabriela pulling close to Carrie. The two of them spoke for a few moments, and Carrie shook her head sharply. I went to the sliding door. At that moment I wasn't feeling anything, just reacting to the shock and adrenaline.

". . . being dramatic . . . so high-maintenance . . ."

". . . she's your friend . . ."

". . . always wants us to swoop in . . . makes it all about her . . ."

Carrie did have some valid points, I had to admit. She turned to me. "Are you leaving too?"

"Uhh . . . no?" I shook my head. "I think no. Hen is passed out on the couch. I shouldn't leave him."

Over by the door, Avani argued with Jessie. The whole scene went into fast-forward, and just like Carrie and Hen had separately predicted, it became the Avani show, with Mari and Jessie clustering around her, telling her this place was amazing, and she was amazing, and she was such a good friend. Carrie watched from the doorway, and I saw she had a tiny hint of the dramatic in her as well, because just when things started to get better, she burst in, stirring Avani up again, and then the two were yelling, and Avani pointed at Gabriela, and Carrie was like, "Hey, you know what, Gabi's actually on your side!"

Pothan and Ken hissed and made catfight jokes, and Avani slapped Pothan, and he came back all wounded and hurt and asked, again and again, why he got slapped.

"Because you were a pig," I said.

He gave me a glassy-eyed stare. "But what did I do? Why did . . . ? What did I do?"

Ken's brain was also turned off. He pounded Pothan on the back. "Dude," he said. "Dude."

Avani gathered all her stuff and pulled Mari and Jessie out into the driveway behind her.

"Wait . . . ," I said. "Why is Mari going with her?"

"Umm, I think Mari is driving?" Dave said.

"What?"

"Mari's the only sober one."

"Dude. Come on. Mari's leaving?"

Now it was my turn to chase down Avani. I followed her into the driveway, closed the door behind me, and spoke in a loud whisper. "What're you doing?"

"Going home. You can *have* the place. Just clean up tomorrow."

"But you're taking Mari."

She blinked at me and at Mari. "So?"

"So . . . I mean . . . she was one of the people who wanted this party."

"She's the only one sober enough to drive."

"Avani, why're you just running away?"

Now her jaw clenched, and her whole body compressed. "I

just don't wanna be here anymore. You stay. Have fun. But, umm, try to keep the place in one piece. And clean up tomorrow."

We heard the distant sound of Pothan's shouts. The flood-lights on top of the garage threw half of Avani's face into shadow.

"Look," she said. "They came here ready to party, and you didn't really have another plan for them. What did you think would happen?"

"You were the one who wanted this party."

"The lake house was always your idea. Even last year, you were the one who wanted stuff to be different. It was your party. Your plan. I don't know . . . I can't help you." She shook her head.

Her key was in her hand, and suddenly the trunk popped open.

"Avani," I said. "Stay. Please."

"There's no point." She smiled at me. "You know, you're a good guy, but maybe . . . you're just not really a leader?"

Embarrassingly, my eyes misted with tears, and with phys-ical effort, I sucked them back into my face—I don't know if that's possible, but it really felt like that. I swallowed, and I turned around, not seeing anything.

Mari was in the doorway, holding her bag, and now she stopped short. My first terrified thought was that she'd heard what Avani had said: *You're not really a leader.*

"S-sorry," Mari said.

"Uh-uh," I said. "You don't have to—"

Avani snapped her fingers. "Come on. Let's go."

I stared at Avani with pure hatred in my eyes.

"Just try to have fun," Avani said. "And be nice to Dave. He's a good guy." Then she shut the door.

The trunk popped open, and Mari went around to the back and threw her bag in.

"Mari," I said. "Come on."

She grimaced at me. "It's okay," she said. "I'll, uhh, I'll be back when I've dropped her off."

Then she was in the car, and I saw her fumbling with the keys. Jessie came around too, giving me a blank look, and got in next to Avani. I thought of Dave, sitting somewhere inside, forlorn and hopeless and abandoned, and my blood pulsed with anger.

When I went in, he was standing by the foyer, his eyes not really registering what'd happened.

"Hey, dude," he said. "I was thinking we could go up and—"

I grabbed him by the back of the neck. "I'm sorry." My throat was raw, and the words came out strangely. "I'm sorry."

"N-no," he said. "I'm the sorry one. I know you wanted more."

"It's okay."

Now I pulled back, and I spotted the beers on the table.

"Well," I said. "Let's get fucked up." *You're not really a leader.*

"Uhh."

I got a beer, popped the tab, inhaled deeply. That salty-piss smell was so good right now. But Dave was still pale and with-drawn and leaning against the refrigerator door with both hands crossed behind his back.

"What?" I said.

"Give me one too."

Outside, Carrie whooped, the sound ululating in her throat, going up and down endlessly.

"We should go outside," I said. "We look stupid hanging out in here alone."

"Err, okay, if you want," he said. "Let me just, uhh, get changed?"

"Why?"

"I don't know. People might get in the water, and I like these pants."

"Sure. Whatever."

Now he paused by the stairs.

"Umm," he said. "Did you want to change too?"

I looked down. What I really wanted was to get so drunk I couldn't think. Those words were still rolling around in my stomach: *You're not really a leader.*

"Okay."

He ran up the stairs, taking them two at a time, and I fol-lowed him, much slower. Earlier, when it became clear we'd be spending the night, we'd dumped our bags in two separate rooms, and in my room I put on my swimming shorts and threw my phone into a drawer. There was a brief flare outside the window, and then more whooping. I sat down heavily on the bed. My eyes hurt.

After a few seconds, Dave knocked on the door, holding his bag.

"Umm," he said. "Since Mari's gone, do you mind if I sleep in here?"

"Sure," I said. "Good thinking. It's gonna get crazy later. We can bunker down together."

He looked around, and I could see him wondering if we'd sleep in the same bed, but I pointed to the trundle bed underneath the main one. "Here." I pushed it out with my feet. "There you go. Sheets are in the closet."

He still wasn't changed, I noticed. He pulled a pair of swim trunks from his bag. Then he looked at me and gave a little smile. One hand was on the button of his jeans. My legs were splayed out on the trundle bed, rocking it back and forth. Now he sat down next to the bag, still searching through it for something, and I lay back, closing my eyes, listening to the sound of the lake.

Then his arm brushed mine, and I opened my eyes to see his face coming at me.

"Whoa, whoa," I said. "What's happening?"

"I, uhh," he said. "I . . . Sorry. I'm sorry. I got too close."

"Oh." I nodded. "Oh, okay."

"S-sorry."

"N-n-no," I said. "No problem."

He gave me a smile. Dave was leaning over me, and I squirmed, which sent him shooting to his feet.

"Sorry."

"It's okay," I said. "Get changed. We'll go down."

I stood outside the closed door, waiting for him to be finished, and I suddenly had a weird thought. I knocked rapidly on the door. "Are you done?"

When he said yes I rushed in.

"Dude," I said. "You were trying out Pothan's advice, weren't you?"

"Huh?"

"You did it just like he said. Plausible deniability. Maneuver me up here. Get me on the bed."

The smell of sweat filled the room.

"Sorry, man," he said. "I just— I'm so awkward—I'm terrible."

"No, no, no, it was good. It's just—"

"What?" he said. "What were you gonna say?"

Now I closed the door, and I sat on the bed with one leg wrapped underneath me. "All right, dude," I said. "It's like, here's the thing. What you did? Totally fine. That's great. It usually works. But . . . I don't know. I really don't. With you and Mari, I wanted something better. And that's *my* fault, because I didn't tell you. I just let Pothan say all that shit, and I never told you different. But it sucks to play all these games. I mean there's nothing wrong with it—no—no—no—" Seeing the look on his face, I put out a hand. "There really *is* nothing wrong with it. At least most of the time. . . ."

He still hadn't spoken, and now my eyes flashed. "Just—come on—just sit here."

He took a seat on the other side of the bed, mirroring my position, and I said, "You know, Mari and you. I was picturing, like, you go for a walk by the lake. You hold hands. You say nice things to each other. Totally relaxed, you know. Maybe you don't have sex. Or even get naked. I don't know. I don't know. I don't know."

Now Dave rolled his eyes.

"What?" I said. "What's this expression?"

"If that's what you were thinking," he said, "maybe you could've *told* me? You had this whole picture, and I had access to none of it."

"No," I said. "This all just came to me. I think what I wanted—literally more than anything—was for you to just—" My thumb and forefinger rubbed against each other. "For you to do it right. For everything to go right. For you to . . . I don't know. You're so amazing. And all that shit Pothan was talking about, it just makes you *feel* bad. That's how a person's soul dies."

He coughed. "Well, whatever, I don't need to worry about it now."

"Oh, crap. I forgot Mari ran off. But you'll get another chance. Or I don't know, if not with her, then with another girl.

142

It doesn't matter. It really doesn't matter."

"No." Dave gulped. "I'm, uhh, I'm done chasing her."

He said that so simply that my body opened up, and I put an arm around him before realizing what I was doing.

"It's okay, Dave. It's okay."

"You know, I *still* can't do it," he said. "I screwed everything up. But it's so hard to juggle every piece of it, and then to also pretend like it's easy. And . . ." He murmured something I couldn't hear.

"What was that?"

He spoke again, and again the words were too quiet.

"Dude, I really can't hear you."

"I said"—he gulped—"that I liked you so much. Still like you."

Teardrops hung from his eyelashes, and the moment stretched to eternity. I put out a hand, put it under his chin, and, hating myself for how fake this all felt, I tilted up his head. Then I kissed him very softly.

His eyes went very wide.

And I thought he'd turn me down, say he didn't want to hook up out of pity, but his hands went up, brushing across the hair of my arms, while mine ran down his sides.

12

AS WE TOUCHED, DAVE KEPT murmuring, "I can't believe this is happening. I can't believe you're here."

I had thought that with a guy I might have an easier time getting it up than I'd had with Avani, but it was exactly the same. Eventually, though, I imagined some sexy things and sort of made it work. Him getting me off was awkward and messy and not that great, but I liked going down on him, because I could control everything, and because he gasped and muttered, "You're blowing my mind" and "This is the most incredible thing I've ever felt." I found it a little astounding, because I'd now been with both girls and a guy, and from my perspective I'd always found it sort of meh. Sex was fun but not incredible. But for Dave apparently it was different. Or he was just being nice.

Afterward he climbed on top of me, and we wrestled a bit, kissing each other for long intervals, and that was the closest I came to really enjoying it. His lips were very soft, and I explored them gently with my own, brushing against and sucking on them, until I realized he was ready again.

The night went on and on in a dreamlike haze, until, finally, my jaws and legs tired, I collapsed on my side. "No more," I said. "No more."

He slumped next to me.

"That was incredible."

"Yeah," I said. "For me too."

"So you finally made up your mind?"

I didn't know what he was talking about, so I nodded.

We lay face-to-face in the light of a single lamp, and the sensation from our lips barely touching each other went all the way through my face and down my spine. Downstairs, hell was being raised, and at one point Pothan came and pounded on our door. We stayed silent. He pounded again and then tried the handle.

I grabbed a blanket, threw it over us. But Dave had remembered to lock the door.

"I'm sleeping!" I said.

"Dude," Pothan said, "Carrie lit a boat on fire. It's fucking incredible."

"Shouldn't you put it out?"

"It's made of aluminum or something. Come down and see!"

Shushing Dave with a finger to his mouth, I said, "No. I'm sleeping. Don't hurt yourselves."

When Pothan had stomped away, Dave glanced at his phone. "Wow. Mari is spending the night at Avani's place."

"Yeah, I assumed she wasn't coming back. Is she okay?"

"Mari is *loving* it. And now, apparently, all three of them are playing pinball."

"Oh my God," I said. "Wow. All right."

We eventually reached the best part of hooking up, when you're both starry-eyed and you talk about weird, intimate stuff you've never mentioned to anyone before. I asked when he'd known he liked guys, and his face went red.

"When you kissed me," he said.

"That's incredible. Before that you had no idea?"

"No, not really. If I look back, then maybe I can be like, *Oh yeah, I did like that guy a little too much,* or *maybe I liked that one scene in that one movie a lot.* But no. I didn't even suspect."

"I always thought it was a possibility." I shook my head. "Except then we hooked up, and that threw me off, somehow." Now his eyes wavered, and I quickly said, "But this time it was amazing."

"You're the amazing one. I never thought this would really happen. Like it's really—oh my God, I'm acting so weird—it's really happening; you're really here."

Now I brushed some of the hair out of his face. Both of us were slick with sweat, and my skin felt like a set of clothes plucked warm from the dryer.

What're you thinking?" he said.

"I don't know. I think I might . . . actually be into this?"

Now he snorted. "You say the weirdest stuff."

"Well earlier I was like"—I rushed over this next part— "let's do it for Dave." I paused, expecting to see hurt on his face, but when none showed up, I said. "But now I'm actually excited." Another pause. "Is that okay?"

"Dude. You are so strange. You did *not* hook up just to make me happy."

"But that's what it felt like."

"You were so, uhh, excited, though."

I couldn't explain to him that at that moment I'd been thinking about anything I could possibly think of, just to avoid losing my erection.

"Yeah. Yeah. You're right."

The sun shone through the skylight. The air above was crisp and blue and cloudless.

At some point in the night I'd gotten disgusted by the liquid sludginess of our two bodies rubbing against each other, and I'd pulled away from him, wrapping the sheet around myself and leaving the comforter, so I spent the early-morning hours shivering on my own, holding my arms close to my body, turning over and over, trying to get comfortable.

My head ached, and I lay silently on my back, trying to get up enough spit to wash the sour taste out of my mouth. Then Dave shifted beside me, brushing a sly hand across my stomach, and now I was ready to go again, and it was half an hour before we even spoke a word.

After finishing, I lay on my back, feeling the happy tiredness deep in my bones, and Dave and I stayed tangled up in each other, not speaking, until we heard the bellow of Pothan's voice downstairs.

"So . . . I guess we should go down sometime?" I said.

"Or not?"

Pothan's singsong floated through the house. "WAKE UP. WAKE UP. It's time now to wake up. You gotta wake up. You gotta get up. The time for sleep is done!"

He pounded on the door, and I shouted, "Give us a second."

"Hey, you're still here?" Pothan said. "Where the fuck were you last night? And where's Avani?"

"She left. Mari drove her and Jessie home. Dave and I crashed early."

"Well get the fuck up."

"Just give me a second."

"Who all's still here?"

"Uhh, I don't know. Dave's in here with me."

"Fuck, okay. You know, if someone was missing because they got murdered in the woods last night, we wouldn't know, we just wouldn't know."

Two seconds later he was running through the house, singing his song again, and after a few moments I heard Dave murmuring to himself, *It's time now to wake up.*

"It's a catchy song," I said.

My stomach fluttered as I stood naked in front of him. The ceiling was sloped, and I had to stoop a bit to put on my pants. Underneath us, through the window, I saw a solitary form walking alongside the lake, and I ducked out of the line of sight.

I felt really gross, but I thought it might be weird for Dave if I rushed for the shower, so I put on my clothes and went downstairs, feeling like a smelly, fetid mess.

The living room and kitchen both stank of stale beer from the cans all over the table and the floor. When I went outside, Pothan and Ken were smoking a bowl.

"Where are Carrie and Gabriela?" I said.

Pothan shrugged.

Dave came down and took a seat on a patio chair. Across the lake, we saw two dots walking across the shoreline.

"I feel like we should swim," Dave said.

"Yeah . . . ," Ken said. "Yeah, dude."

Hen came out, rubbing his eyes. "What the fuck?" he said. "What happened last night?"

Ken, maybe too eagerly, pulled out a beer, and Hen waved him off. "Never again," he said.

I, meanwhile, had texted Carrie.

Me: Where are you?

Carrie: Gabriela's mom picked us up.

Wow. Uncool. But I guess they didn't want to be the only girls left.

Looking at the lazy smiles surrounding the patio, I had a vision of us bobbing up in the water, drinking afternoon beers, maybe watching some TV. Dave and I gave each other half smiles.

"I'm totally gonna swim," I said.

"But it's a lake," Ken said. "Aren't there worms and snakes and shit?"

"Probably."

It took a long time to get moving. For ages we hovered on the edge of doing something and doing nothing. Pothan sank into his seat and seemed almost asleep. Finally I ran into the water, feeling like a complete fool, and even Dave took a few seconds to follow behind me. I jumped on him, and my hands ran freely over his shoulders and neck. The bed of the lake was muddy, soft, and gross, and I tried my best to stay off it, but the water wasn't as completely frigid as the ocean would've been.

We dove and resurfaced, the water clanging in our ears. I kept expecting Pothan and Ken, or at least Henry, to join us, but they didn't. I could imagine Avani and Mari sitting out on the pier, wearing their sunglasses, arms drooping as they leaned backward, trying to catch the sun. It didn't strike me as weird that all the girls had withdrawn, but it did make my heart ache. For the first time since last night I remembered those words: *you're not really a leader.*

Dave swam over to my side. "What's wrong?" he said.

"Nothing."

"You sure?"

"No, uhh, let's see what the guys are doing?"

They were in the living room, watching a San Francisco Giants game—we were in the division playoffs.

Ken and Pothan didn't even look away from the action. Hen nodded at us. "Sorry," he said. "Was just about to follow you."

"Water was nice."

In the shower, my head vibrated with anger. Fuck them for not coming into the water. No, no, I couldn't think that way. Something was wrong with me. I was way too angry.

Dave met me outside the shower. He was still shooting me worried looks. "What's wrong?"

I shook my head. "I'll see you downstairs."

All three guys were on their phones.

"Fuck these high school bitches," Pothan said. "I say we head out to Santa Cruz tonight."

Ken looked up. "I could do that."

"Break into some house parties?" Pothan said. "You remember that time at the frat party, Nandan?"

"Umm." I shrugged. "Sure."

Hen ran a hand through his hair and gave us a lazy smile. "Not for me."

"Come on," Pothan said. "There'll be paaaaalenty of guys in Santa Cruz. Paaaalenty."

Now Hen gave a shy smile. "You won't abandon me?"

Pothan sat straight up. "No! I am appalled. You really think I'd ditch a bro?"

Henry shook his head, but the gesture apparently meant yes instead of no. "All right, fine. But let's at least get some Advil."

"Daaaaaaaaaave?" Pothan said. "You're the oddest man here, but you shouldn't be the odd man out. Come on. Let's find you a bitch to replace that bitch."

"Huh?"

"Your girl? The one who abandoned you? Get back on the horse, dude."

Now Dave looked at me. "Uhh, sure."

"Not me," I said.

Pothan rolled his eyes. "Dude."

"No. I want to go home."

"Dude," he said. "Santa Cruz is in the opposite direction of home."

"Dave has a car."

"But he's coming with us."

"Take Ken's car. You don't need two."

A few minutes later, Pothan pulled me into one of the side bedrooms. "Dude. What the fuck? Why are you getting in Hen's way?"

"I have no idea what you're talking about. Hen can still come with you. That's fine."

"Dave. The little guy has gotta be queer, right? I mean that's why he asked about anal last night. And that's probably why he never closed things with his girl. So . . . I mean . . . let's put three and five together. That equals eight, dude."

"Umm, okay, that didn't make any sense, but I'm sorry. I don't think Dave's—" I stopped for a second. Actually, I had zero clue whether Dave would be interested in Hen. But that was even more reason for keeping him away. "He's gotta drive me home."

I bullied the guys into cleaning the lake house, then Dave and I said goodbye and drove east on Highway 17. Dave was at the wheel, and I couldn't help squeezing his thigh.

"Stop," Dave said.

My hand crept higher. "What?"

"You'll get me distracted, and I'll crash this car," he said. "Seriously."

"Then pull over."

There are a few driveways and back roads that cross 17, and we stopped in front of someone's tall hedge, making out furiously in his back seat, grinding against each other. And now, when I couldn't do anything about it, I was painfully hard, and every motion of his hips sent sparks shooting across my eyes.

Afterward he said, "I don't want to stop hanging out."

"Oh, we're not gonna," I said. "I just didn't want to go to the boardwalk."

"Y-yeah. Okay."

I punched him in the shoulder. "You knew that."

Now he gave me a sad, sideways smile. "But I really didn't. I sort of thought that last night was . . ."

"A one-time thing?"

"Yeah. And that's *fine*. I don't expect anything more."

"No, dude," I said. "I think it'll happen again, but we shouldn't be awkward. I don't want this to be like me and Avani."

"What was it like with her?"

"Nothing like this."

"Y-yeah?"

"No, I don't think she even liked me."

"That's crazy. Of course she liked you. She still thinks you're amazing. As a friend, at least."

"No." I shook my head. "Not even as a friend."

"Then why would she hook up with you?"

Now I was treading on dangerous ground, because I knew exactly why you'd hook up with someone you didn't like. I knew that sometimes when you're alone in a room with someone, and they want you so much, sometimes you say okay just so they'll be happy. "Girls do that sometimes."

"Well," he said. "So . . . so how are we going to be different?"

"I don't know. We'll keep being friends. We'll keep caring about each other. We'll keep—we'll say what we mean."

"I'm okay with that. And if you want to hook up with other—with girls—that's fine."

That permission was priceless, and I should've hoarded it,

but instead I spoke instinctively to wipe the strain off Dave's face. "You don't need to worry about that."

"So . . . what now? Should we go to your place?"

"No. If we keep being alone, we'll just keep hooking up, and it'll go on until we both die of dehydration. We have to be around other people."

"The beach?"

"No . . . too many people who know us."

Another silence. I heard the grinding of gears in his brain: *Oh, so it's a secret. Well, of course it's a secret.* And I totally understood that weirdness, because until this moment I hadn't really thought about the "staying closeted" aspect of it.

Then Dave said, "If, uhh, if I had, uhh, mentioned to somebody that you and I had hooked up at your apartment, would, uhh, would that have been a problem?"

"Who?" I said. "Hen?"

"Err . . . it's . . . uhh . . ."

A hummingbird flew through the hedge, hovering briefly in front of us, then flitting upward and out of view. "Come on, dude, the suspense is killing me."

"Mari," he said. "It was Mari."

"WHAT?" I said. "What the fuck? When?"

"Err . . . so remember we were at GameStop, and Hen was *so* awkward about stuff? Well outside the store she was like, 'So are you gonna kiss me?' and I was like, 'Uhh, actually . . .' and it all tumbled out of me."

155

"You're kidding. So she's known about it the whole time?!"

"I asked her not to tell anyone." Dave's knee jogged up and down.

"Wait . . . so . . ." I narrowed my eyes. "What're you not telling me?"

His lower lip pulled down, showing just his bottom teeth. "I might've planned a little caper. . . ."

"Dave," I said. "Dave . . . Dave. Dave. DAVE. Are you telling me that this was all a scheme to get with me?"

"Err . . . I am a master criminal?"

Now I grabbed his face and pulled him close, kissing him on the lips. "I love this. Dude! That is awesome! Wait. . . ." My forehead got tight. "Ken and Pothan weren't in on it, were they?"

"N-no-no. Just Mari."

"But not Avani?"

"No."

"You're sure," I said. "You're totally sure Avani doesn't know. Because something about last night is suddenly making a little more sense." Now I remembered—Avani had mentioned Dave right as she was leaving.

My fingers were on my phone. Avani picked up in a few seconds.

"Tricked!" I said. "I've been tricked!"

"Hey, dude," she said.

"I'm here with Dave," I said. "And he just told me a verrrrrrrrrrrry interesting story."

There was rustling on the other end, and I heard some very hysterical giggling.

"Err, am I on speaker?"

"Jessie's here too," Mari squeaked.

"Oh, like she wasn't in on it too . . . ?"

"Hey." Jessie's voice piped in quietly. "In on what?"

"You know what," I said. "You three . . ." I looked at Dave, then I squeezed his thigh. "You four . . ."

"What're you talking about?" Avani said.

The laughter caught in Mari's throat, and I imagined her in Avani's basement, lying on a couch, her body vibrating like jelly as she tried to keep in her excitement.

Avani and Jessie kept denying knowing anything, and at one point I muted the call and told Dave, "You haven't told them about last night?"

He shook his head. So I took the call off mute, and I went around and around with them, grilling Avani, trying to see if she'd known anything about me.

"Okay, okay, okay, I told them!" Mari said. "Now, did it happen?"

"I am appalled," I said. "You *outed* me. You outed Dave. This is my privacy. This is my safety. This is my—"

"NANDAN!!!" Mari yelled. "I—AM—GOING—TO—DIE."

"Well, I don't know," I said. "Dave. What would you say? I can't believe they haven't asked you to report back yet."

"WE WERE GIVING HIM HIS SPACE."

Dave looked oddly unamused. His lips twitched. I said, "Thanks for the info, Mari," and abruptly ended the call.

"What's wrong?" I said.

He shook his head. "She told them about me."

"Dave," I said, "people gossip. The moment I told Hen, the clock was ticking. I told him. You told somebody. They would've told other people soon enough. Nothing stays secret."

"But it's really not cool. I mean, you joked about it, but they *outed* us. People, like, die from that sort of gossip."

"Yeah, but we're not gonna die, are we? I mean are your parents the honor-killing type?"

"I can't believe you're so okay with this."

I turned over his palm, feeling all the muscles on the inside of his wrist. He hadn't minded at all when I'd told Hen, but this was obviously a bit different. Or maybe it was only different because she had done it and not me.

My phone had been buzzing and beeping ever since I'd hung up on Mari, and I finally answered.

"You're being summoned," Avani said. "Both of you. I think Mari will actually have a stroke if you don't tell her what's up."

"Sure," I said. "We'll come down."

Dave was quiet on the way over, until I slipped a hand through the gate of Avani's mansion and found the tiny button that opened the electronic lock.

"Umm," he said. "This doesn't look—"

"Don't worry. This is how I do it."

I went around the side and down to the basement door, expecting her to open it right away. But we waited for thirty seconds, and, instead of knocking again, I called her.

"Where are you?" I said. "We're at the door."

"No you're not," she said. "I'm at the door."

"At the basement door?"

"What're you doing? Come by the front."

So I took Dave around again, and we walked up between two big marble pillars and rang the doorbell. Avani, looking tiny against the gold and marble of the foyer, threw open the door. We heard distant giggling upstairs.

"Hey!" She hugged Dave first, and his lips twitched. Then she came in to hug me too, and I pulled her bony body close.

"Awesome," she said. "Come up."

The stairs curved in two wings, leading to the mezzanine level. She climbed the stairs, trailing her hand on the flowery wallpaper, and took us to a massive bedroom. I mean this room was easily bigger than the living room of my apartment. There was a canopy bed in one corner, a love seat tucked into one bay window, a sitting area clustered around the other one, and a little open area on the floor near us where beanbags and folding chairs were clustered together.

"You're here!" Mari shrieked. She jumped up, seemingly coming out of nowhere, and ran at me shoulder first. I oofed as she hit me, and my arms wrapped around her. "You smell good," she said.

"Err, okay?" I said. "Are you all right?"

When she pulled back, her eyes were wide-open crazy. "WHAT HAPPENED?"

Mari was in tight yellow high-waisted shorts and a blue tank top, the whole outfit totally unlike the jeans she normally wore.

"AVANI DRESSED ME," Mari said.

Jessie flowed upward from a chair by the window, and when she slid closer she said, "Hey."

"Hey."

Now Mari was clinging to Dave, and she tried to get him bouncing up and down. Avani had a hand to her mouth, and the two of us exchanged smiles.

"What is going on here?" I said. "Have you guys been drinking?"

"I think she's just excited," Avani said. "Uhh, hey, you can sit down."

I collapsed onto a beanbag, and then I grabbed Dave's pant leg, telling him to get down here with me, and we huddled together on the edge of the cushion. Avani sat cross-legged on the floor, while Jessie sat awkwardly on her hands.

Mari dragged over a chair from the corner. "I don't sit on the floor," she said. "I'm not a floor-sitting type."

"So, uhh, what's been going on here?"

At that, Dave gave me an openly beseeching look. I'd promised him this would be a short stop.

"Well, it's been half about you, of course," Avani said. "And the other half about that *disaster* last night."

"Oh yeah," I said. "I forgot. That was crazy."

"Carrie was so wild," Avani said. "I don't know *what* has happened to her."

"Yeah," Jessie said. "She's really not like that."

"Well . . ." I shook my head. "I mean she wasn't when you were twelve."

"No," Avani said. "I know this isn't politically correct or whatever, but it's this gay thing. It's so totally about image for her. Like if you guys suddenly started, I don't know, to lisp and wear crazy clothes, it'd be an act. That's not you."

Dave looked monumentally uncomfortable, and I was almost angry with him, because it'd taken me *so* long to get into this room and have these conversations.

"So she's dead to you," I said.

"Well that's what we're discussing," Avani said. "Do we give her another chance or what? I mean, she and I have been friends for ten years. That's pretty incredible."

"No, I know."

Jessie's soft voice interjected. "And she's fun. You like her, Avani. You know you do." Jessie looked at me. "I think we're just hurt. We can party too." Her smile was sad. "But Carrie doesn't think about us anymore."

"Come on," I said. "She wouldn't even have *gone* to the lake house if she didn't care."

We circled around, talking about Carrie and Gabriela and the events of last night. Dave came in a few times for some teasing from Avani, mostly about his complicated and round-about plan for getting with me. He smiled at these jokes, but he looked bored and uncomfortable most of the time, and I found myself wishing, on some level, that he wasn't there.

Finally I saw him yawning, and I told the girls we had to go. Avani looked up through her lashes. "You sure? I have a pullout."

"In this room," I said. "There's a pullout?"

"Yeah, that couch. It pulls out."

"For what?"

"Umm, for this?"

Dave shook his head, and I told them no. It took another thirty minutes for us to break free. The whole group followed us to the stairs and to the door, and it was only when my hand was on the doorknob that Mari burst out with "But you haven't told us anything!"

I winked at her. Dave was sort of curled inward, looking at his shoes.

Then we were out the door. The sprinkler system was on, and a fine mist hit us in the face as we walked down the path. In the car, Dave finally took a breath. Then he looked at me with a sad, expectant look in his face.

"So you did it," he said. "You got into the inner sanctum. Now if you just want to be friends, that's okay. We can—"

I kissed him.

13

OVER THE NEXT TWO WEEKS, Dave and I hooked up constantly. Usually it was at my place, on nights when my mom was at work, or at his place, before his parents came home.

The sex usually started out great. I was excited. I was into it. I enjoyed kissing him, but when we got to more intimate things, I tended to get a little bored, and almost always I had to picture somebody or something else in order to finish.

More and more, I sidetracked things by going down on him. Weirdly (to me), I enjoyed that a lot. It was sort of relaxing. I could control the pace. He gave me lots of positive feedback with his gasps and moans and frequent repetition of "You're blowing my mind" (it was basically his sexual catchphrase). And most important, I didn't have to be so anxious about whether I was enjoying it or not.

And, okay, whatever, maybe that was normal. Maybe I was a bottom? (Isn't that what they call the goer-down-on-er? Unlike Hen, who seemed to have been born with an understanding of what all these words meant, I still hadn't really even cracked open my big gay dictionary.) And I *could* and *did* get off each time, eventually. But something about our sex left me feeling damp and unclean, as if I was covered in a thin layer of spit. I'd travel outside myself and look at the two of us with our long ungainly bodies grunting and huffing on the bed, and it would just disgust me, and the only way to get through it, I kept finding, was to imagine Avani.

She came more and more into my mind as I hooked up with Dave. Sometimes, when he was trying to get me off, I'd imagine her body underneath me, my hand resting on her hip. Other times, when I was going down on him, I'd stare up into his eyes and imagine I *was* her, that I was inhabiting her foxy, narrow face and looking at him through her pale green eyes.

Somehow in all the haze and anxiety of trying to get it up, trying to finish, trying to make him happy (because he wanted to make *me* happy), I'd gotten to this place where every time we hooked up, I had to include Avani somehow in the fantasy—the whole situation worried me, and to be honest I mostly tried to shove it out of my mind the moment the sex was over.

Anyway, the part afterward was the best. We'd lie together,

and our lips and hands would run over each other while soft words passed from mouth to ear.

One time Dave pressed his face to my neck for a long time, and I said, "Are you crying?"

"No." The word was muffled.

"Then why is my skin wet?"

He pulled back, wiping his eyes with the back of his palm. "I'm sorry. It's just this is so crazy." The words piled up in his mouth. "I feel like my body is exploding. It's actually painful. It's too much. I understand now why people get stressed out, why they break up with people they l— like. I get all the drama. I get everything."

Hearing him, I actually got envious. I wanted to feel that too. Now his hands brushed across my side and my chest, and I was getting worked up again, which was what *always* interrupted our talks, and I took both his wrists, holding them to one side.

"What are you saying?"

"Just that I'm not good enough. You're, like, a solar storm. You're a jet engine. You belong with somebody like Hen. Another special person."

"Dave," I said. "I'm not with Hen. I don't even like him that way. You're the person."

"For now," he said. "But I'm just practice for the real thing."

"Come on, it's high school. Isn't it all practice?"

He gave me a weak smile. And in his eyes I saw something

else. This wasn't practice for him. When he looked at me, he saw us welded together forever. College, marriage, growing old. The love from movies and songs.

I let go of his wrists. His face got pinched and sad. "I didn't even get to practice. You did everything for me. Made every move. If it wasn't for you, I'd still be alone." Now his eyes went to the shelves all around us. "That's something I think about a lot. How you just pointed a finger and picked me."

"Yeah, of course. Because you're awesome."

"Am I?" he said. "What's awesome about me?"

"Well . . . you're cute," I said. "And hot. And smart. And a really good friend."

"Mmm-hmm, but I don't have that extra thing," he said. "That edge. The thing *you* have that forces a person to love you. And that's okay. I'll get it someday. You've taught me a lot. You don't owe me anything."

After that I held him for a bit, and, of course, we hooked up again. In the days after, I tried to write a text message to Dave where I put into words exactly what I liked about him. Because he *was* different from other people—not just other guys, but girls too. Some silken thread connected the two of us, and if I could only name that connection, then everything would be solved. And I *did* send him a few texts, but they all seemed slightly wrong. Because he wasn't the bravest or most handsome or most stylish guy I knew. And although he was smart and nice, I wasn't sure those were the things I cared most about. But when I thought about him, I felt this throbbing in my chest, and that was something, that was *real*.

If only I knew whether I really was gay, I'd understand it better. Dave assumed this was just my intro to some grand new bisexual life, but I didn't see it that way. More and more, I felt like a straight guy having a solitary queer adventure.

Ironically, this made me push the sex harder than he did. Because while for him it was a fun pastime, for me it was about figuring shit out.

I pirated a few books about gay sex and read deeply about all the stuff we could do. Then I made pleading eyes to the clerk at a feminist sex store in Palo Alto, who I'm sure imagined me stuck at home with a pair of dragon-like Indian parents who would disown me if they found out, and she let me buy some stuff. When I brought out my purchases, Dave was really shocked. He was happy with the sort of things we were doing, but I wanted to go further—to have *real* sex, by which I meant anal sex. All the books stressed that sex didn't have to be penetrative to be real—but that was just words. I needed to know if I was capable of enjoying this.

I couldn't get hard enough to enter him—I just bounced right off—so we decided he'd enter me instead. The first time was really painful. It burned a bit, and I kept feeling like I had to go to the bathroom—but after we'd done it a few times I realized that was normal. He seemed to enjoy it a lot, and I enjoyed the feeling of being connected to him, but afterward I always wondered if there shouldn't be more to it than this.

When I first had sex with Avani, I also hadn't enjoyed it very much—the whole thing was a lot of worry and anxiety, all for a pretty mild payoff. But I'd thought maybe that was because she and I were new to it, and we were always drunk, and we weren't comfortable with each other.

After Dave and I happened, at first it seemed like this eureka moment—*Oh yeah, the reason sex with Avani never clicked was because I was gay!*—except it never really clicked with Dave either.

I tried talking this through with Mari, but she was all like, "Hmm, do you think you might be asexual? You can still be with Dave if you're asexual! You could be a biromantic asexual, you know. Or you could be a demisexual!"

And no offense to Mari, but I changed the topic pretty quickly. Because all that stuff just felt like words. Whenever I tried to talk about what was actually inside me, I felt as if the world's answer was *Well, if this is what you're feeling, then here's a word for that!*

But I *did* want to have sex. I *did* look at porn. I *did* masturbate. (And when I did I mostly thought about women.) Except with Avani, the sex wasn't good. And she was hot! And I hadn't been able to make a move on Hen. Maybe I hadn't liked him? But with Dave everything had come so easily! And when I thought about him, it was hot too. Except when we were actually together, I could only get off by thinking about Avani!

Now maybe if I looked online I'd find some sort of word for that, but did that matter? I didn't need *words*. What I needed was to know: Is Dave the right person? Or should I try to sleep with Hen? Should I do other sex stuff? Or keep doing the sex stuff I've been doing? Or not do any sex stuff at all?

And at the same time there was this other question: *Who do I want to be?*

Because I did know that having or enjoying sex wouldn't mean anything to me if it turned me into an outcast. Back in the, like, nineteenth century there were guys who openly had sex with other guys, and they risked getting beaten up or killed for it. And there were probably lots of other guys who were kinda willing to try it, but they were afraid, so they kept those feelings pent up forever, until they died. And I knew, without question, that I would have been one of those latter guys.

If getting with Dave had entailed even a small risk of being bullied or abused, I wouldn't have done it. I'm not saying that today is perfect. There are lots of places where a gay kid can still get murdered or at least thrown out of their house. But that wasn't here, now, this town, my school, my home. Here, at this very particular moment in a very particular place, being queer was sort of cool.

And part of me wondered if that was why I'd done it.

This summer I'd been Pothan's lackey and Avani's former

hookup. But if I came out as queer, I'd be somebody entirely different. I'd be able to come to a party alone, without feeling out of place. My queerness by itself would put me into a separate category. I'd be able to text anybody, talk to anybody. Sometimes the thought occurred to me that maybe I could become the premiere person in the Ninety-Nine: a Pothan without the douchebaggery; an Avani without the drama; a Hen without all the sneering irony.

Already, Avani and Jess and Mari and Hen treated me differently. The moment he learned I was queer, Hen became my buddy. Mari now spent plenty of evenings texting with me or hanging at my place. And Avani and Jess had finally cut me into their group chatting (which was mostly complaining about Carrie, but whatever, I was down for complaining).

I was pretty sure if I came out, everything would change for me. My role in the world would be so different. Not to mention that maybe the sex thing would change too! Maybe the reason I wasn't enjoying it was because I was anxious about coming out. Or maybe I actually was queer, but I wasn't attracted to Dave.

Except even that didn't feel right. Because sometimes, especially when we weren't in our houses, like when we made out for hours in his car, I'd get flushed and excited and filled with crazy, wonderful emotions that I couldn't put into words. One Saturday night I laid my head on his chest and murmured, "Thank you," again and again.

His voice rumbled through the bones in my head and chest. "For what?"

"Making this happen," I said.

"I didn't do anything."

"You made the lake house happen." I said. "You knew I wanted it, and you made it happen. You got Mari lined up, and she lined up Avani."

"Y-yeah—I mean, I thought it'd be funny—like you were helping me, but meanwhile I'd help you—"

We were in the back seat of his car, surrounded by the darkness of the forest. "Well okay, now let's think: I've gotta pay you back. What can I do for you?"

He shook his head. "I don't need anything."

"Do you need someone to build you a rocket to Mars?"

"Well, yes, but I wouldn't trust one that you made."

We laughed, and I made fun of him for being nerdy, but right at the moment when he might've gotten offended, I switched tacks, rubbing his chest, and asked him to tell me all about it. To be honest, I got bored when he gave me the details of his Mars Club projects, but I liked his arm around me; I liked the sound of his voice. I didn't understand people like him, who cared about things other than who was friends with whom, and who was in and who was out, and, essentially, who was popular. To me, high school was the entire world. Listening to him talk about his plans for the future, a coldness crept across my back.

"What's going to happen to me, Dave?"

"Huh? What do you mean?"

"Like, am I shallow?"

"Nooooooooooo, of course not."

"Dave!" I pushed him away. "You think I'm shallow."

"Well . . . you're interested in different things from me."

"Yes, shallow things."

"You're the one who keeps saying the word."

We talked then, about me and him, and he reassured me that I wasn't shallow, but he couldn't really explain why that word didn't fit. He said I was kind, that I saw into people's souls and cared about their true selves. But I wasn't sure that was true. He said I was smart too, and that definitely didn't seem true. But what came across was that he really, really liked me. That to him I was the combination of every good thing in the world.

"You know"—he gulped—"if, uhh, if I could choose between going to Mars and, uhh, this thing with you? I'd choose—"

"Don't say it! You'd choose me? Bullshit!"

"No." He blinked. "I would. . . . I really would. . . ."

Something in his voice left me feeling warmer and happier and more excited than I usually did, which meant that when he dropped me off, I was for the first time completely sure that I wanted to be with him.

14

THAT NIGHT, WHEN I WALKED into the apartment, my mom was in the kitchen, listening to the Bollywood radio station. She works nights, so on her days off she usually doesn't sleep well, and she's always happy to stay up with me.

"You're home!" she said. "Should I heat some water?"

We drank tea at the kitchen counter. She asked how my life was going, and I mentioned something funny that Mari had said in class earlier.

"You and this girl, you've grown very close."

I laughed. "Mom. You're so bad at this."

"Well, I am only saying that I like this new girl. She seems . . . studious."

"Avani was studious."

"No, she wasn't."

"Mom, it's true."

"A girl like that doesn't have good grades. Have you actually seen her grade reports? How do you know she wasn't exaggerating about them?"

"Mommmmm," I said, feeling like a kid again.

My mom has a way of asking questions where she circles around back onto things you think she's forgotten about. She picks and picks and picks, without ever revealing her true thoughts. That's what she did about Mari. There wasn't much light in the kitchen, just the dim glow of the table lamp, and my mom's round face took on a strange and sickly color in the darkness.

And although I *knew* how to stonewall her—deny, deny, deny, as many times as you need to—I couldn't help this time, in the intimacy of our twin cups of tea with their many lumps of sugar, giving out little hints about my love life that she then jumped upon and pursued.

So I told her, very guardedly, with lots of stumbling and pauses, that I'd kind of started seeing "my friend . . . a guy friend—Dave—remember . . . I told you about Dave?"

She took it with her usual blank face, but a few seconds later she gave me a hug and said, "Thank you for telling me, and of course it doesn't matter, and can you please invite him over sometime?" And afterward we got emotional and nostalgic and talked about how she and I really needed to spend more time together!

I kept expecting, and fearing, she'd ask something like

"How long have you known?" And I wasn't sure how I'd answer. Even now, this felt unreal—part of me still considered it a joke or a trick, something to shake up my life—and when she finally left to go to sleep, after a while my whole body started shaking from silent laughter. I fell into bed, stuffing my face into the pillow, and, not knowing if this insane feeling was real or if I was playacting, I convulsed as the air gushed out of my lungs and into the fabric of the pillow.

The next day I told Dave I'd come out to my mom. He excitedly asked if he could tell his parents too, and I was like whatever, sure. He had to study all day, and my mom was at work, and I was all alone on the couch, browsing on my phone.

Mari texted me an "I'm sorry," and I texted back a question mark.

Mari: Just apologizing for how I've been acting since you guys got together. I went a little crazy, and Jessie said it might've been a little objectifying.
Me: Don't worry about it.
Mari: No but seriously, she said you guys seemed uncomfortable.
Me: Lol, don't believe Jessie. We're fine.
Mari: So let's not talk about Dave. What else is new?
Me: I came out to my mom last night.

The pause lasted for just a moment.

Mari: WHAT?!?!?!?!?!?! DOES THIS MEAN YOU AND DAVE ARE BOYFRIENDS?!?!?!?!?!?!

Me: You're amazing at staying cool. Just amazing at it.

Mari: HOW DID SHE TAKE IT? WAS IT HARD?

Me: It was totally fine.

Mari: CAN I COME OVER? WE HAVE TO TALK ABOUT IT!!!!!!

Mari bounced into my apartment with an excited gleam in her eye. She jumped onto the couch, looking very much like a little sister, and gave me a dreamy sigh. "What a weekend."

"So you're still hanging out with Avani?"

"Yep!"

"And she's still pretty mad at Carrie?"

"So pissed!" Mari said. "Lady Macbeth angry! So much crying! But she and Carrie had like a little peace summit at the mall today. It was so cute. I swear my eyes turned into little hearts like an anime character."

"Do you need to do your homework or something?" I said. "You clearly got nothing done today."

"Uhh, no, right now, we're gabbing," she said. "Time for a gab sesh."

"Oooooooookay."

She grimaced. "I mean unless you don't want me here. . . ."

I got up, shook out my shoulders and legs, and restrained this weird urge to go loping around the room and hooting to myself like a monkey. Instead, I flopped onto the couch, and she, uninvited, curled up next to me, burrowing into my side.

"So . . . ," she said. "What happened with your mom?! How did she take it?"

"Fine. It was cool."

"Why'd you come out? Why now? Did something happen with Dave? Are you gay or bi? Does he know? What does he think? Are you gonna tell anybody else? Will you come out at school? How about Hen? Hey, does Hen know?!"

"Hold on, hold on, hold on," I said. "Umm, it was pretty sudden. Just an impulse. I don't enjoy feeling as if it's a secret. About school, I don't know. . . ."

We went through her questions at extensive length, and it was unsettling to be the focus of so much personal attention. Mari was willing to talk forever about the details of my life. I had no answers for her, not even about my own emotions and my own plans, much less about what my mom or Dave must've felt, but she seemed happy to soak in the bath of my own confusion.

"Hey, by the way, how did you two actually get together at the lake house?" she said. "Dave gave me zero details."

"Umm," I said. "Well . . . it was funny, actually." I told her about Pothan's sex advice—she shrieked again ("You mean all that advice was for hooking up with *me*?")—and I told her the way Dave had lured me upstairs and tried to make a move.

"And it worked," she said.

"Yep, I guess."

"How do you *feel*?" Mari said. "When I first told her, Avani was so like, *No, no, no, Nandan comes off that way, but he's really not gay*, then we talked about it a whole lot, and she was like, *buuuuuut* he did—"

Mari stopped suddenly.

And maybe I should've felt awkward, but she was so guilty and quiet that I said, "Err, yeah, I had trouble getting it up with her. But that happened with Dave too. It's normal. It happens."

"THAT'S WHAT I SAID. I was offended on your behalf."

"How would you know?"

"I know things. TV. Books. I read. I know things. Guys get nervous."

Now she was jittery and achy, I felt her heart pounding next to mine, and I wrapped my arm tighter around her. We sat in silence, and I just wanted to slow things down, because all of a sudden so many sights and sounds and impressions had crashed into my brain. I felt tears come to my eyes, and a sudden weight pressed down on me. My head went into her curly, voluminous hair, and I sniffed slightly. All of these crazy thoughts had struck me: *I don't want this. I'm not queer. This isn't me.*

Maybe Mari noticed I was crying, or maybe she didn't. Her arm wrapped around my trunk, and the two of us now were hugging each other very tightly. "I bet Dave was so happy."

"Oh—" I cleared my throat. "Oh yeah?"

"He really likes you."

"That's what he said."

She shifted, leaning back, and from this angle her eyes were two half crescents of white. "He did?"

"Yeah. Right before it happened. That's what he said. Actually it was, 'I liked you so much.'" Saying the words, a shiver ran through me, and I remembered Dave's eyes, dark and wet, with twin dots of reflected light in his pupils. "It was really nice."

"It's insane," she said. "That it actually happened. He and I talked a lot about it. Everybody has that crazy inaccessible crush, but his actually *happened*. It *happened*. Like, in real life, when you want somebody that bad, it never really happens."

Her words calmed me. I thought of Dave, scrambling around in his house, calling his parents together and giving them this terrible shock. He might be doing it tonight. And all because of me.

"Hey, hey," I said. "I've gotta call him."

"LOL," she said. "Okay. Maybe I'll actually do work."

"He's coming out to his parents *tonight*. I am such an idiot. I am so self-centered."

"WHAT?!"

"Err, yeah."

She got up, jumping for her phone, and huddled in a corner. I told her not to text anyone about any of this, and she looked extremely pathetic, staring at the useless phone—I eventually took it away from her, but she pulled out her computer instead—while I texted Dave.

Me: What's up? How's it going?

Dave: Mom just got home. Waiting for her to change clothes. Then I'll get her and my dad together. Only want to do this once.

Me: Will it be a big deal?

Dave: No.

Dave: No.

Dave: Not really.

Dave: No.

Finally he wrote:

Dave: Okay, it's happening.

Me: You want to talk?

Dave: It's okay.

I had this crazy temptation to write back *I love you*, but I didn't, thank God. Mari and I waited, in cold silence, broken by fits of laughter, and she joked it was like an execution. I sat in my chair, riven by dread.

Finally my phone lit up with a call.

"Hey," I said. "How'd it go?"

"Oh, fine," he whispered. "They lectured me about AIDS. Said to be absolutely sure I was safe, because there might be deadly consequences. Asked me if I was sure. All that stuff. I, err, might've told them about you, but they sort of ignored that part."

"Are they listening right now? Why're you talking so quiet?"

"Yeah they're outside. It was just so weird."

"Oh no," I said. "I'm sorry."

Mari looked at me with a hangdog expression, and I, not saying anything, went into my room and shut the door behind me.

"It was weird," he said.

My eyes drifted to an old sound system sitting high up on a shelf. The black grilles of the speakers had a blank, menacing look.

"It was really weird," he said again.

"But tell me, was it weird?" He didn't laugh at the joke, and my stomach collapsed.

"I don't know. I don't feel great. Sorry. This was so easy for you. But I'm not like you."

"No," I said. "No, come on."

"I can't explain it," he said. "They were totally fine. They were like, we love you and everything. But it was weird. I guess this is why I'm me and you're you."

"Dave," I said. "Stop. It's okay to feel strange."

"But you didn't," he said. "You were so brave. You just went for it."

"So did you!"

"Only because I had to."

We talked like this, going around and around, and my heart swelled. The pressure inside my body was intense, and I had a physical yearning to be there for him, to kiss him, to hold him, to make him feel better, but instead all I got was his hollow voice, ringing out, quiet and unsure, into the silence of my ear.

Eventually he yawned and said he needed to work. I promised we'd see each other the next day, and he said, "It's okay. You've done enough. I know you're not my, umm—" His voice clamped down on the last word, but I understood it.

"I'm— I—" The words *I love you* were the only ones I had, but they didn't come out. "You mean a lot to me. You're *so* brave. I'll see you tomorrow."

When I came out, Mari's face changed from happy and joking to concerned. She shrank back into the couch. "What happened?"

"It was okay. Everything's fine."

I couldn't describe the unsureness and the sorrow I'd heard in Dave's voice, so I didn't. Instead, I smiled at her and joked about his parents, saying they'd given him a talk about AIDS. She gasped, saying, "Oh my God, really?" And she was horrified, but her horror was tinged with laughter, and Dave's hadn't been. There'd been nothing funny about that phone call.

I felt the narrowness of my escape. I'd almost let Dave go through that alone. I'd almost stayed away. And for no reason, just because I hadn't thought to do it. My hands gripped the plush sides of the chair, and I took a deep breath, holding it for fifteen seconds, before letting the air out in a thin hiss.

* * *

The next morning, some part of me thought the whole school would already know about Dave and me, but even Carrie, when I ran into her, seemed to suspect nothing.

Dave and I met for lunch, sitting maybe two inches closer than would two guys who had never kissed, at the same table, far out by the lemon trees, where I'd gone and talked to him a few weeks ago, and, to my surprise, my whole body tingled from his nearness. Maybe I actually *was* queer. Maybe I really did like him. This was exhausting; I was so tired of questioning myself.

"Hey, are you okay?"

"Yeah, totally," he said. "I was just being stupid. Everything was fine."

"Your parents act weird again?"

He shrugged. "They're okay. What about your mom?"

Ants swarmed over a lemon that'd fallen onto the edge of the table. With a backhand motion, I smacked it onto the field.

"I think this news made my mom really happy. I guess she thinks gay guys get into less trouble," I said.

"Umm, but . . . are you gay? What exactly did you tell her?"

"I told her I was seeing you!" I said. "That's the beauty of us"—I waved my hands between us—"of this thing. No explanations needed."

"Are we an 'us'?"

"Well, that's what we should discuss. To be honest I've been considering the benefits of being 'out.'"

The word felt artificial to me, and I made a face.

But he picked up on a different word: "You're so weird. The 'benefits.' I know you're not really that unemotional about it."

Now I looked into Dave's brown eyes. We were two people who were bound together for eternity. Just like a first crush or a first kiss, a first gay hookup is a milestone that sticks with you forever. But were we anything more than that? Could I love him? Could I love anybody? I'd loved Avani, I thought, but probably that had been something else: a combination of envy, gratitude, and disbelief.

"I don't want to be myself anymore," I said. "I want to be different. And this coming-out thing is a way to do it."

"See, most people would say: 'I want to be my real self.'"

"But that's not how I feel—that's how other people feel, but not me. To me, it's like—it's like—it's like I am the thing people see. When Pothan chose me, when Avani hooked up with me, I became something different. Before them, I was a nobody. Afterward, I had a role."

"You were always golden."

"Not really. I was pretty shy."

He shook his head. "No, trust me. You were always something different. I used to watch you, moving through the parties, and everybody knew you, everybody was friends with you, everybody trusted you. I'd try to remember what exactly you *said* or *did* to win everybody over, but the words would go blurry in my mind. I don't know. You were awesome."

A spark ignited in my chest, and a voice said, *What if he's right, what if I am something special?* But just as immediately I rolled my eyes. "Thanks. That's not true, but it's a really nice thing to say."

Dave adjusted the tips of his bow tie. Between us and the school, kids played soccer on the long, damp field.

"So, uhh," I said. "If we went public, how would you feel?"

"I'd be ecstatic. That'd be awesome. But we should also, like, talk things through. None of this stuff needs to be so fast. I mean, I totally get what you're saying, but people will like you either way, and we should—"

"Why wait? I don't want people to say I'm closeted. I've *never* been closeted."

"Okay, well, so do we just . . . tell people? Or we could do an Instagram post?"

"No, no, no. That's not how it's done. You might be college-level in math, but your rumor-spreading skills are stuck back in kindergarten. The way it's done is that you tell your friends to tell other people. That's how Hen did it two years ago. He didn't want the hassle of coming out again and again, so he told me to tell everybody. Now he gets to return the favor."

"You know I don't need you to do this."

"But I want to."

"And you're serious?"

I nodded. In that moment, I was absolutely sure.

15

HEN MUST'VE GONE TO WORK immediately, because by that afternoon the coming-out was proceeding with unstoppable force. I'd already gotten a dozen texts about it, and I'd answered none of them. The whole thing—so simple at lunch—had turned into a grotesque spectacle.

After school, Pothan rammed into me on the sidewalk, jumped on my back, and yelled in my ear, "Dude, you and Dave?"

I staggered and rocked back and forth, trying to keep my footing. He hung on to my back, his head tucked into my neck, and said, "My baby Nandan is all growed up."

Finally, I bashed his body against a telephone pole, and he dropped off and wrangled me into a hug. "You weren't gonna *tell* me?"

"Umm . . . ," I said. "Yeah, I guess I should've . . ."

His smile flickered between proud, embarrassed, and smug. "I bet you *love* the attention," he said.

That made me laugh. "That is such a microaggression. It's definitely at least a medium-aggression."

"Come off it, bro," he said. "I know you. I know my little Nandy-poo. He's always working the angles. He knows his shit."

Now I smiled. "You motherfucker. Okay, okay. I don't know, maybe . . ."

"You love it."

"Well," I said. "Part of me does. But the other part—"

"No, you love it. You totally love it."

With that, my smile faded. Pothan didn't want to talk to me about anything *real*.

"What're we doing here?" he said. "Should we celebrate or some shit?"

"Waiting for Dave."

"You told your mom yet?"

"She was fine with it."

Dave walked up, and Pothan pounced on him too, and we went through the whole thing again, except this time he also kissed Dave on both cheeks and said, "Welcome to the family, bro."

He wanted to take us for a ride, but we finally managed to leave him at the street corner, still shaking his head to himself.

On the way home, Dave didn't try to take my hand, thank

God. He actually never touched me when we were in public, not even to hug.

In the week or two after the coming-out, only my mom asked the question I'd been dreading: "So how long have you known?"

I said, "As soon as I knew anything, I told you." And that seemed to be enough.

I thought Avani at least might ask more. Maybe she'd say, *Oh, when we were together, were you confused?* Or *Was this why you couldn't get it up sometimes?*

From her, I would've loved those questions, but they never came.

The coming-out (if that's what it was) took astonishingly little time. Within a week everybody in my life seemed to know. Mr. Radherec, my precalc teacher, was gay, and he stopped me after class to say if I ever wanted to talk, I should come to him.

"Sure," I said. "Thanks."

"But you're already seeing someone, I hear." He shook his head. "Kids today. It's so different. I only ever dreamed of that."

I thought of Henry, and I wondered if it really was very different at all.

Hen texted to invite me to a GSA meeting. I said *maybe*, and he was like:

Henry: Yeah, it can be a little awkward, but it's sort of important for at least one of us to represent. Otherwise it's all queer girls and str8 ppl (and ppl who're pretending to be str8 allies but're actually closeted, god bless them).

Me: Sure, I get it.

Henry: How's it been? Have the girls started _touching_ you? For me that came almost instantly after coming out.

Me: Lol, no.

Henry: It'll happen. You're kind of the chief gay now.

Me: No. Come on.

Henry: Yeah. It's not a title you can refuse.

Henry: Do well by my people.

Me: Uhh, are you all right? Are we good?

Henry: No no we're okay. But remember you still owe me that favor!

The weirdest thing wasn't the coming-out. That was tense and awkward, but it made sense. The weirdest thing was how quickly everybody changed their mental vision of me.

Random girls—people I'd never spoken to before—started laughing at my jokes, seeking me out, confiding in me. Guys also changed. A lot of them were awkward. Aside from Pothan, who seemed determined to prove how normal he and I still were, a lot of the physical joking-around stopped. Guys didn't hit me in the shoulder or wrestle with me. They also didn't make fun of me in the same way. I wasn't "one of the guys" anymore.

But I also wasn't a girl. They still weren't careful with me or my feelings like they were with a girl. None of the guys imagined that I might be into them. If anything, they treated me like a person without any gender at all.

Yet I also had terrifying shamanic power in their eyes. Ken in particular seemed both drawn to and put off by me, and one night I got a call from him, where he without warning launched into a story about this girl he'd had sex with, and they hadn't used a condom, and now it sort of itched down there, and he wondered if he had crabs or something.

"Might just be dry skin, dude," I said.

"Yeah, but I've looked and looked and sometimes I see black stuff. . . ."

"Umm, I don't know, but I'm googling it, and I think crabs are tiny bugs. They're not just specks. What color are your pubes?"

"They're sort of a light brown, like my hair, I— What? Does it matter?"

"I don't know. Mine are black, but if yours are light, then they'd probably be easier to see in there. Unless what you've got are chameleon-crabs. Want me to take a look?

"N-no."

"Because I'll look."

"No! Dude, I just wanted to know what you thought."

"I dunno. My mom's a nurse. Should I ask her?"

"No. . . . God, come on."

"Well, then, I don't know what you want from me."

Guys respected my opinions more. It was like I'd stared into the darkness and seen things that man (emphasis on *man*) was not meant to see, and though the experience had marked me as an outcast, I was at the same time protected and empowered by that knowledge.

These were the things I said to Mari one day, when she was at my house studying for the precalc midterm, and she said, "Wow, that sounds intense."

"Not really. It's just weird. I'm something different now."

The two of us were sitting on the sofa, right above the spot where Dave and I had first hooked up.

"What does Dave think?" she said.

"I don't know. We haven't talked about it."

"Really?" she said. "He came out too. Wouldn't the same thing be happening to him?"

"Dave's different. This is less of a change. He's always come off as a little—uhh—separate."

"Not to us."

I shook my head. "Uhh." This was Mari's first mention of her initial crush on Dave. "Yeah. Not to us."

"I can't believe you haven't talked about this. You two have been spending like every second together."

My stomach ached at that too.

"Yeah . . . but that's basically all hooking up."

"What?" Mari sounded both excited and scandalized.

"Time we spend alone without engaging in sexual stimulation is, well, pretty minimal."

Mari's laughter was slow to start, and it continued, nervous and spastic, for a few seconds.

"Sorry," I said. "Was that too much?"

"N-no," she said. "But you guys are such a stereotype."

"I don't know. I don't know. I don't know. It's so weird. Like . . . this is about sex. It's sex. That's all it is. Basically I went out and announced—'Here's who I like to have sex with!' and people were like mmm-hmmm, yessssss, that's very interesting. And yet it means something. Somehow it means something to them, this thing with Dave and me."

"It's not just sex, though," she said. "You like him."

"Sure. But I don't know if we're in love."

"And that's normal."

"But with him it's so ordinary. It's like—okay, you know what it's like? Imagine if you and I were having sex. We'd do it, and then we'd play around and make fun of each other, and it'd be really *simple*. That's me and Dave."

She blinked. Maybe I'd gone too far. "Well, you're welcome, by the way. This is all me. I put together this whole caper. This whole plan. This whole 'pretending to be together.' All me! Don't believe Dave when he tries to take credit."

"Yeah. . . ." My jaw worked. "Thanks."

Now she blinked at me. "Are you mad?"

"No," I said. "Not at you. It's just that everybody is so

happy. There's this crazy rush to lump Dave and me together, as if we're married or something—and it feels like, well, it's good those two fags are taken, because now we don't have to think about them too hard."

Now her mouth opened. "Uhh, no. . . ."

I shook my head. "Not you," I said, even though she was absolutely guilty of this too. "You've been cool. But it's in everybody's eyes. To them we're a single unit."

"I thought you liked him!"

"Sure, sure, but . . ." I shrugged. "I don't know. When I got with Avani, it was really exciting. I thought about her all the time. I dreamed about us getting married and shit. With Dave it's different."

"And that's okay."

"Yeah, sure," I said. "Except . . . what if I don't even like guys? What if it's just a phase? I thought if people knew we were hooking up, that would be one thing, because that's a *fact*. But people took away something different."

We went around and around, talking over my feelings, in that deliciously pleasurable way that's like picking at a peeling sunburn. Dave texted he was on his way over, and I told him Mari was here.

Dave: Oh, uhh, should I not come then?
Me: What? No. Just letting you know.

When he appeared there was a bit of awkward shuffling as the two said hi. He threw his bag onto the floor and sat on a couch, far away from me. I guess we hadn't really hung out with anybody as a couple, and we had no idea where to look or how to act.

For her part, Mari looked at me, then looked at Dave.

"No, no, stay," Dave said. "I need to do work."

"Yeah," I said. "You know this kid does three hours of homework every single night?"

Mari closed one eye and looked at me quizzically. "What do you mean? How much do you do?"

"I don't know. Half an hour?"

"Are you serious?" she said. "No . . . you're kidding."

"What's there to do? You do the problems, and you do the translations or whatever. Maybe I'll read for an hour or two if there's a test tomorrow. But what else is there?"

Dave said, "This guy's basically a genius. He doesn't even take notes."

"I never got into the notes thing. It's all in the book anyway, right?"

"Yeah, but you take notes on the reading too . . . ," Mari said.

"Why, though? It's all in the book. It's right there, written down already."

"Err . . . in order to learn it?"

I shook my head. "I mean don't get me wrong, I knew people at this school did work. But I figured those were, like, you know, the kids who you hear about at announcements, the ones who win science competitions and have 4.0 GPAs and shit, not ordinary kids like you and Dave."

"Uhh"—Mari's forehead crinkled, and she raised an eyebrow—"I have a 5.1."

"See?" I said. "What the fuck? That's insane. How is that even possible? So you get straight A's *and* mostly take honors classes?"

"Err, your friend Avani does just as well."

"Yeah, but she makes sure you know it."

"Well, anyway, I'm here to, like, genuinely work. So if you guys—"

"No, no," I said. "Let's do it."

After half an hour I was done with my homework, and I started texting and fooling around on my phone. But eventually I stole a glance at Dave and Mari, and I realized the two were completely lost in their reading.

Dave was in his bow tie, as usual, and looking at him made my stomach drop (in a good way, definitely in a good way). His hair was slicked over to one side, and his body formed one long sinuous curve. Mari looked up, noticed me staring, and gave me a merry smile. Dave never looked at me like that. His eyes always held something brooding, sad, and a little bit anxious.

We hadn't quite defined what we were to each other. Everybody thought of us as boyfriends, I knew, and Mari once used that word, talking about us on the phone to her mom—she said, "Oh yeah, Dave is Nandan's b-boyfriend, I guess," although she grimaced at me while she said it.

The word made sense. We did spend a lot of time around each other. I started coming over openly to his house, although his parents were weird about things. One afternoon we timed things wrong, and his dad opened the door to the basement, sending us scurrying into the storage room, where Dave called up, "Hey, I'll be out in a second," as if he were alone down there.

A few minutes later, the two of us appeared upstairs, and his dad didn't breathe a word about why Dave hadn't mentioned I was at their home. I'd met both his parents by then, and they knew Dave and I were together, but they still treated me like an old friend who'd dropped in for dinner. They didn't ask me anything about myself—not a word about my studies or my plans or my activities—and instead just included me in their table banter about politics and television. Whenever Dave and I mentioned spending time together or having plans, they got a strained look and skipped over the subject as if I hadn't said anything.

My mom's response, on the other hand, was more awkward (though less painful). She rushed up to Dave and grabbed his face and hugged him really deeply and made jokes about how he was "civilizing" me. She got his telephone number, and if she wanted to know where I was or how I was doing, she actually texted him! He in turn texted her once when he had a stomach-ache, and she rushed to his house, without me, to see if he was okay.

In comparison to Avani, whom she'd always loathed, she openly praised Dave and even asked what his college plans were and whether we'd considered going to the same university.

I did actually like the sense of being settled. And I really liked, oddly enough, meeting his friends! Dave had a whole circle of nerdy Mars Club friends who met twice a week in a room at school. Dave was the president of their club, and they were well into developing their proposal for the Mars Society annual meeting.

They didn't have any overt reaction to Dave's coming-out, but their interest in me was sweet, innocent, and very undisguised. They were like a litter of puppies crawling over each other to investigate some shiny new object. One guy in particular, who obviously worshipped Dave, sat next to me and explained, in his nasal monotone, everything Dave was talking about, and afterward the guy volunteered to work with me on the day's project.

I made some jokes. They weren't my best, but they went over pretty well, and in general I enjoyed the complete lack of judgment or difficulty. They already liked me, just because I made Dave happy, and whenever I had lunch with them, they accepted me without problems. But their conversation was always about superhero movies and obscure science fiction stuff, like downloading your brain into robots or the possibility of a killer AI arising. At times I laughed, not thinking they were serious, but they didn't even notice.

Eating with Mari's friends was more awkward, but much more fun. The awkward part was that they didn't understand who I was or even the concept of the Ninety-Nine. They were just three friends who'd met freshperson year and ate lunch together each day and liked to talk about their lives and their crushes and what videos they'd recently watched online. They weren't isolated, precisely, but they were *so* much tighter with each other than with anybody else. And I think when Mari and I talked about people like Avani, or about the parties we'd gone to, it aroused a strange sense of jealousy in them, as if we were saying we were better than them.

I learned to redirect the conversation, to ask about them and their shared history, to say nice things, to text them, and to slowly work my way into their group. And that was pretty easy. They were open to having me around, and a few times I even ate with them when Mari wasn't there, although when I explained to Avani what I was doing, she was very confused. But I just liked them. Hanging out with Mari was one of the unexpected bright spots of this year—I couldn't even say where or how our friendship had started—it'd appeared out of nothing.

For her part, Mari hung out with Avani whenever I was

with her, but she acted like a tourist who was content to go home when her visa ran out.

"Don't you ever want to be closer with Avani and her crew?" I once asked as lunch was breaking up.

"No, not really. They're fun, but I have my real friends."

"Wait? Am I one of the fun ones?"

"No!" She jumped up, grabbing me around the waist, and hugged her face close to my chest. "I mean yes! But you're one of the real ones too!"

Despite all the practice with Mari's friends, I hadn't quite worked my way into Avani's inner circle. Part of the problem was that I was shy. I was afraid to ask her to do anything with me, because I knew the first no would stand between us forever. Now that I was queer, it was like our entire previous relationship was wiped out, and I didn't want to mess up our blank slate.

One night Avani called me out of the blue to extensively discuss the merits of some guy who was camped out at her Instagram, liking all her photos, and I sat in my room, smiling to myself over how natural all of this felt.

The Avani thing made zero sense to me. The thought of her sitting in her house somewhere, legs crossed, holding the phone to her head, made me insanely happy. But I suppose lots of people get weird friend crushes. Or at least I told Mari about it, and she was like, "Whatever, that's normal."

But for some reason I stopped mentioning Avani when I was around Dave.

16

ABOUT A MONTH AFTER THE lake house, I was in
the midst of hooking up with Dave when I had a thought that
couldn't be resisted: *I am really not enjoying this.*

The thought stayed with me even as we kissed and cuddled
and touched. I didn't want this. I'd done everything possible to
convince myself this was a natural fit, including coming out to
the whole effing world, but it still didn't feel right, and now it
needed to *end.*

I told myself to chill out. I'd done this dozens of times, and
it would be over soon. But whereas before it'd just been slightly
boring, now every touch was torture.

The words *I don't want to do this anymore* floated to the top of
my brain, and I barely held back from saying them. After he left, I
took a shower and played a mindless mobile game and finally fell
asleep. The next morning I woke to a long string of heart emojis

from Dave and, to my relief, I felt happy. When I saw him at school, he smiled broadly, and while he talked I stared at his thin lips, trying to understand whether I actually liked him.

We sat together at lunch with Pothan and Ken—not touching, of course, but still next to each other. Pothan took the floor, laughing and joking and mocking Ken for his outfit, saying you can't wear a blue shirt and blue jeans—you look like a fucking Smurf. Then Jessie dropped by, asking about our homecoming plans—clearly, she wanted to know if this year the Ninety-Nine would be headed to homecoming or if we'd be sitting it out.

"You know I just love letting Ms. Felcher smell my breath," Pothan said.

Our school had a zero-tolerance policy for drinking at dances, and the entrance to homecoming was a receiving line of teachers who shook our hands and stared closely into our eyes and tried to detect if we were drunk.

"Come on," Jessie said. "You can be sober for *one* night."

"Maybe I can't," Pothan said. "Maybe I'm an alcoholic. That's a medical condition. You can't discriminate."

Jessie rolled her eyes. "You know I *dream* sometimes about being at a school where the boys aren't such idiots."

"Hey," I said.

"Oh, not you," she said. "You're one of the good ones."

"What?" I said. "That's absurd. I demand to be lumped in with the bad ones." But secretly I was happy that she thought I was different.

She looked at me and Dave. "Hey, are you guys going?"

I shrugged. "Umm, if people go, I shall go; if they stay away, I shall do likewise."

"You are all sheep," Jessie said. "Ugh, we are so pathetic."

This year we didn't have a Lyle to keep us away from the party, and I *wanted* to stand up and be like, *Fuck this, I'm going*, but I remembered that feeling a month ago of going into the lake by myself, wondering if anybody would follow me, and then trudging back into the house to find I hadn't really been missed.

As the lunch clique broke up, Dave said, "You know, I'm fine going to homecoming with you."

"Yeah, but do you *want* to?"

"Sure, I guess. I've never had, like, a date to a dance before. I don't know if it'd be awkward or . . ."

"No. . . ." I blinked a few times. "No. . . . I think that's fine."

"Well, you can think about—"

"No, no, no, we'll do it," I said. "I'll—ahh—I'll buy tickets?"

"You sure? I can buy them."

"It's okay. I'll do it."

At the time I was like, whatever, we'll go to homecoming. But a week passed, and I didn't ask my mom for money to buy the tickets. I had the half-formed idea that maybe Dave and I would break up before the dance even happened.

I'd met Dave because he was always standing at the edges of T99 parties, but that was in the past: nowadays he hung out more with his nerdy friends, and when I asked what he wanted to do on the weekends, he was always like, "Spend time with you."

This Friday he texted to say:

Dave: Hey, can we actually not hang out tonight? I really need to get this stuff done for the Mars Club.
Me: Sure. No problem.

I hadn't gone out in a while. Somehow I couldn't imagine Dave and me together at a party. What would we do? Would we talk? Would we kiss? Hook up? It was easier to just not do it. But tonight I was alone.

When I texted Pothan to ask what was happening, he replied:

Pothan: About time you came back to us!
Pothan: Ken's parents are gone. I think we were gonna hang out at his place.
Me: No girls are gonna want to come to Ken's basement.

I'd forgotten this part of things. How you spent most of the night not actually at the party but staging for it, hanging out with your guys, waiting for something to happen, or not happen. And I didn't want to do that anymore. At least, not with them.

Pothan: What do you care?

Me: Lol, I'm gonna see what Avani's up to.

Pothan: Just because you're gay now doesn't mean you're not still my dude, dude.

Then I texted Avani, and she said their plan was to hang out in Ken's basement.

When I showed up at Ken's, everything was forgiven. His basement wasn't actually a basement; his house was built above ground level, and there was a rental unit (currently empty) tucked into the area underneath. The ceiling here was low, and Pothan's head was six inches from touching it. Between drinks, he put his hands on the plaster of the ceiling and heaved upward, like he was carrying the world.

The room had barely enough space for the kitchen and a couch. People were spread all across the floor, and Pothan had jacked up the music so you could hardly hear, but I was having a good time.

During my absence, new members of the Ninety-Nine had appeared: little freshpeople and sophomores brought along by their friends, or crashing the party, awkwardly holding cups and looking around with frightened faces.

I was instantly at home. Pothan grabbed me by the shoulders and tried to press me into his drinking game, but I evaded him. Carrie hugged me and said, "What's up, dude? I haven't seen you in a while."

"Nothing much."

I smiled at her girlfriend. "Hey, Gabi, surprised you came back."

She shrugged. "Just here to keep her out of trouble."

"Hey, so has Jessie roped you into this homecoming thing?" Carrie said. "She's really on me about that."

"I guess so."

"Whatever. The moment Avani says she's not gonna do it, Jessie will cancel too. She's such a follower. I don't get it. Like, she has zero life."

Normally by this point in a party, Pothan would've hollered at me to disrupt my conversation and pull me back into his orbit, but as a gay guy I was safe. I saw glances at me from all the corners of the room. Kids knew who I was, and although the feeling was uncomfortable, I also thought, *Well, hey, I kind of deserve this.*

More than anything, I loved the sense of warmth. I had a place here. I wasn't dependent on anybody, I could come or go as I wanted. I could even sit alone in a corner by myself, and people would know it was by choice, and not because I had nobody to talk to. I had power. And, yeah, it was less than Carrie's or Pothan's, but it was still real.

This was demonstrated the moment Avani walked in. Nobody understood better than Avani how to dress for the California fall and still look good; she was in high-heeled boots and skinny jeans, and there was something in the cut of the clothes and the layering of colors that set her apart from the other girls—and the guys too, of course, though aside from Pothan, with his leather jacket and side-swept hair, they weren't even trying.

But she had no power. Most guys knew Avani didn't hook up, and something in her eyes froze out even the younger boys who would've crushed on her anyway. Her power had always lain with her girls, but in this room they were either like Carrie, too loud and too outgoing and too drunk, or they were younger girls, hanging on to attention from guys who barely noticed them.

She hugged Carrie, and she was polite to Gabriela, but then Avani's eyes flicked across to me, sitting on the edge of the couch, and relief blossomed in her face. It was a weird thing: She and Carrie didn't *like* each other, but they were friends. Whereas Avani and I weren't really friends, even though we liked and respected each other.

She came to my end of the couch and prodded my elbow. I slipped sideways, scooting into another girl. "Oh hey, sorry," I said.

"It's okay." The girl was young and unformed, with a tiny face and sticklike arms. She leaned forward, her eyes wide.

Avani said, "Hey, what's up?"

She was propped on the arm of the sofa, where I'd just been. "Where's Dave?"

"Studying. Jessie?"

"Same, but with a guy."

"What? Jessie likes a guy?"

"Yeah, some random dude."

"Who?"

"His name's Niko?"

"Diamandis!" I said. "You're serious? The unicorn!"

The girl next to us leaned over, listening.

Avani laughed. "What? You know him?"

"Remember Hen mentioned him once? The fanny pack?"

"Well, I've never seen the fanny pack, but what the hell? Yeah, I looked through his photos, and I was like 'He's *not* hot,' but Jessie was like, 'Umm, he is demonstrably hot, I am not alone in this.'"

"I know Niko." The voice piped in, small and sweet, from somewhere around my armpit.

Avani's eyes got tight, but I sat back so the girl could lean into our conversation.

"Oh yeah?" I said.

"We were in a play together."

I felt Avani's tenseness, but she leaned in over my shoulder. "Oh, hey, what's your name?" The girl instantly gave her heart to this friendly older girl, and in the process forgot all about me.

Avani might've temporarily lost out to Pothan, but she had the tools to make a new power base. There'd always be girls hungry for her approval. Even if she was alone and by herself, Avani carried power in her walk, in her clothes, in her makeup, her voice, and the sheer force of the I-give-zero-fucks attitude that she carried with her all the time. She was everything a girl was supposed to be, and if she liked you, then somehow you got to keep a tiny bit of that power for yourself. I remembered a year ago and a party just like this, where the touch of her eyes transformed me from a nobody into something bigger and stronger, half girl and half boy—she'd given me a piece of her power, and sometimes all I wanted was for her to say, "You did a good job, Nandan. You really did."

But now Avani was pulling her games, fawning over the sophomore girl, giving her compliments, and asking about her other friends, and I knew this would go on for a long time, the way it always did, with Avani treating me like just an accessory—the guy she needed by her side to look legit—and I shook my head, getting up to see who else was around.

Except in a moment Avani was with me again. "Hey, where'd you go?"

"Nowhere. You seemed like you were getting along okay."

The girl was still on the couch, alone, staring at us with covert eyes.

Avani took my arm. We were in the swirl of the party, but people made space for us. "Hey," she said. "You want to leave?"

"Umm, to do what?"

"I don't know. Hang out. We need to catch up."

Her half smile briefly turned into a full one.

"Sure," I said.

There was no way to leave quietly, so we picked our way through the party, taking everybody's eyes with us, until at the last minute Pothan took back a piece of his power by shouting, "You already turned him, Avani. He's on the other side now!"

The room was too loud to shout back something witty, so she gave him dagger eyes and a middle finger and slammed the door behind us.

17

AVANI'S HOUSE WAS VERY WARM, and it was hotter as we went up the stairs, hands trailing on gilt banisters. In her bedroom, she hopped into one of the chairs, tucking a foot underneath herself.

Already on the way back she'd raged against Pothan, calling him a pig and an asshole and asking how I wasn't more pissed at him.

"He's fine. He didn't mean anything."

"You were right, you know," Avani said. "He was the enemy. I didn't see that. I thought it was Carrie."

"'Enemy' seems like too strong a word."

"But do you remember?" Avani said. "When you tried to sell me on your capers? That was so fun. *That* is what we should've been doing this year. Not hanging out in Ken's basement."

A strange woman—a maid?—came in carrying a tea tray, and she set it down on the coffee table between Avani and me.

"He's *gay*," Avani said. "He's gay. He likes men."

"Oh, uhh." The woman blinked at me. "Hello."

"Hey."

"Tinu-Auntie thinks I'm still twelve years old and need to be watched around boys," Avani said.

"I just know what rules your father has set."

"We'll keep the door open. It's okay, Tinu-Auntie. Trust me."

The woman left, not without a backward glance, and I heard the slow creaking of the door as she checked to make sure it wouldn't swing shut.

"So, uhh, how's stuff?" I said.

"I don't know!" she said. "Something is wrong with me. I'm just so fucked up. The other day I looked through old pictures of me and Carrie, and I *cried*. And not just a little bit. I cried like a psycho."

"You were good friends," I said.

"And your gay thing . . . ," she said. "I don't know. Can we talk about it? Is that okay?"

"Yeah, totally. . . ."

She put a hand to her head and made some motion that wrapped her hairband around her wrist, letting her ponytail fall free. She shook it loose, and I watched her gleaming skin, her face, and the slightly off-center look in her eyes.

"I don't know," she said. "It's been weird. Like, I made you.

Transferred a little bit of my power into you. As if you're my Horcrux or something."

"You're incredible."

"What?" She blinked. "Did that offend you?"

"No, I was literally thinking this exact same thing. How you made me."

"What happened to me? Last year was so different. Like, was that an illusion? We had everything."

"It was *not* an illusion. You were incredible. Everybody loved you."

"I know; I had power. I woke up, and life felt exactly how it's supposed to feel—I mean, you know that night we hooked up?—I was just like, I'm tired of these guys, none of them are worthy of me. Not a single fucking one. I'm better than this shit. So I chose you."

"You never told me that."

Her voice was faraway. "After I had you, I was untouchable. Nothing could hurt me."

What seemed incredible was that the two of us could've ever kissed, could've ever hooked up. Seeing her now, her coat and poncho and boots and scarf discarded, sitting sideways in her seat, with one hand passing through her hair, I thought she was so regal, such a queen.

My skin vibrated, hearing those golden tones in her voice, and I pushed myself back into the chair to avoid seeming too amped up.

She talked about old parties—things we'd done and seen together—and I laughed at her stories. She gave me a new perspective, talking about guys who'd tried shit with her, and how she'd always managed to put them off or outwit them—the ways she'd used her relationship with me, maneuvering through me or around me, bringing me up at just the right moment—and I saw how our relationship was only one element of a larger plan.

She opened up, laughing more often, showing the whites of her teeth, and she relaxed into the couch, tucking both her feet under her.

"So that's why you came and grabbed me out of Pothan's car that one time?" I said.

"Yeah," she said. "Yeah. I needed to distract Lyle. He could be so creepy."

I didn't know what to say. I'd hated Lyle, and I'd been afraid of him, but Avani was talking about something different.

"Except sometimes I wonder—and I know this isn't the feminist thing to say—but maybe he's what I needed. This year it's so tame. I stay at home, and I think, *Oh, whatever, what are we missing—just another party; Pothan running around being a joker*—the thing is he doesn't *need* me. Lyle needed me somehow—Pothan doesn't care—I don't know, I don't get it, I'm not sure what changed."

"Maybe you should try some college parties."

"I don't know. Fuck it, maybe I should just go to homecoming."

214

Her voice dripped with loss and longing, which was strange for me, since right there, with her, in her room, I was experiencing so much joy. She checked her phone, typed something briefly, and my heart stopped, thinking she'd want me to leave, but Avani said, "Jessie texted. I said you're here, and now she wants to come over."

"Sure. I love Jessie."

"Yeah." She shook her head. "You know, I always thought Carrie and me were the real friends. Jessie came later, but she stuck around."

We talked a little more about Jessie. Avani and I scrolled through Niko's pictures together. His feed was moody and over-the-top, full of these soulful photos with books and waterfalls and trees.

"Do you go for this?" she said. "You said Dave liked him."

The words *I don't know, I might not even really like guys* were on the tip of my tongue, but I didn't say them. It'd taken me so long to get into this room.

"Having a boyfriend," she said. "That must be so weird. Like, yeah, of course you're going to homecoming. That's what you do with boyfriends." Another swirl of her wrist locked her hair back into its ponytail. "I've never had one."

Suddenly she looked at me, and her eyes overpowered mine, sending my gaze to the ground.

"You know it's not great for my reputation to have dated a gay guy."

"Err . . ." I grimaced.

"It's not a big deal, but people do laugh. Especially if they know how we got together. I guess this is why a girl should always let the guy make the first move."

"Uhh, I'm sorry." My face was burning.

"I should've guessed. You always really wanted to sleep over, to meet my friends, come to the lake house, do all that girly stuff."

"Yeah," I said. "So you got that?"

"No, I don't know, I didn't think of it at the time. Somehow it, like, made sense. I thought it was cute."

This was the conversation I'd wanted to have with Avani for the last year, but now a sense of dread surrounded us. Rain fell across the dark sky, and my eyes alit upon the light from the two electric candles set into bronze wall sconces.

"When's Jess getting here?"

Avani laughed. "Hey, what's going on with Hen?" she said. "Why didn't you go for him? He liked you."

"I don't know. He's a lot to take."

"Dave." She shook her head. "I would not have guessed that."

"He's really nice. I don't know. With him it was easy."

Avani untucked and recrossed her legs, leaning over to the other side, and we talked about Dave for a while. She asked me questions about our sex life, as easily as if we were discussing normal stuff, and I spilled, saying sometimes I had trouble

216

getting it up, just like with her. I expected her to pick up and run with that, but instead she darkened and changed the subject. I told her how awkward Dave's parents were and how my mom loved him so much, and she was like, "Yeah, I don't see why you didn't come out earlier, dude, if your mom was so cool with it."

I shrugged. "I didn't know."

"So when you and I . . . ?"

"No, I, umm . . ." This would be the moment, probably, to tell her that I did like girls, that I mostly liked girls, that my thing with Dave was an experiment, and not a successful one, but I didn't. After a few minutes the front door opened, and Jessie came in, smelling slightly damp but beaming broadly. She plopped herself onto the beanbag chair and said, "Finally, this happened!"

"Jessie was always a fan of yours," Avani said.

I smiled and winked at Jessie. "So, what're we doing for homecoming?"

"Uhh, going?" Jessie said. "I'm gonna tell Niko to ask me. I'm just doing it."

Avani frowned, as if unhappy, but then she laughed. "All right, if you ask Niko, I'll make Pothan take me."

The introduction of Pothan into the mix made me frown, but I said, "Sounds good, let's do it," and within an hour I'd pulled up the school's website on my phone and bought tickets for both Dave and me.

The rain continued well into the night, right through the midnight meal where Avani's dad ordered pizza and questioned me pointedly about my life. After dinner, I stayed at the table, wondering when and how I should leave, but Avani and Jess retreated upstairs, and I timidly followed. When Avani's dad checked in, she answered again by saying, "Nandan's *gay*," and he left us behind.

We dissected Jess's conversations with Niko—he was so indirect, never allowing himself to be pinned down, until finally Jess had to come out and text "Will you go to homecoming with me," and even then he was just like "That sounds cool," and we had to assume that meant *Yes, I will go with you to homecoming.*

I was going to walk home, but with a glance in my direction, Jess said, "Oh, just stay on the pullout. We still have plans to make anyway." Inwardly, I cheered, grateful for all the times I'd tried to get on Jess's good side.

But when we were in bed I felt a sense of wrongness. The two girls were on the same mattress, whispering to each other, too low for me to hear. I was exactly where I wanted to be, but I was here under false pretenses. I had no doubt that if they weren't 100 percent sure I was gay, they wouldn't have wanted me here. And yet, wasn't it true? I was dating a guy. We were exclusive. According to Henry I was king of the gays, long may I reign. So maybe that's who I was.

The next morning the girls didn't really get going until, like, ten, when we all went out to Valley Creamery for breakfast. All the time they were on their phone, sending out loose tendrils of connection to other girls, and I did the same, thinking I'd text Carrie—I was pretty sure I had more pull with her right now than they did—and when she joined us at the creamery with Gabriela in tow, I felt I'd scored a small victory in Avani's eyes.

Breakfast turned into coffee down the street. We rolled over to my place to pick up some gym clothes for me, then back to Avani's house, where we worked out in her home gym. School-books appeared, and I stared at my notebook, afraid to reveal I wasn't really doing anything, and feeling all the while so overwhelmed and like such an impostor. I was sure that I should leave, and yet I badly wanted to stay.

That night, we convinced Avani to come out, and she spent an hour getting dressed, letting us veto outfits, then changed back into casual clothes and wrapped her party clothes in a bundle. I left first, and Jess and Avani rolled out second, pretending they were going to Jess's place, and picked me up at the corner. We went and changed at my apartment, and then appeared as a little pack at a house party down the street, where Avani for the first time in ages acted somewhat like her old self. She swanned across the room, made a big scene, shot sardonic looks at all the guys, then pointedly ignored them. And all the while Jess and I played the role of handmaidens, just like I once had for Pothan, except this time I genuinely enjoyed it. Just seeing how people greeted her, how excited they were, how they hungered for her approval, and how they laughed at everything she said, I knew she was something so much bigger and more glorious than I could ever be.

About this time my phone started to blow up with texts from Dave. He hadn't seen me since yesterday, and he was miiiiiiissssing me. I wanted to tell him we'd get together tomorrow, but he said he'd come to the party, so he showed up, in his bow tie and jacket, with his awkward smiles, and Avani and Jess gracefully withdrew, like real bros, to let him and me hang out.

Of course, after half an hour, he got nervous and anxious, and somehow we ended up in his car, headed for another night of my trying to enjoy his groping and fumbling. He touched my thigh while he drove; I felt a wave of disgust that made me think, *Oh, so this is what normal guys feel when another dude touches them.*

"Hey," he said. "What's wrong?"

"Nothing."

"Are you sure?" he said.

"No, I'm fine."

"Sorry I wasn't ready to party. You seemed like you were having fun with Avani."

"Yeah, we spent the day together. It was actually really cool."

"Oh."

"You don't really like her."

"She's good. It's just that she can be a little . . . self-absorbed."

"But that's the beauty of her. I don't know. I can't describe it." My gaze went distant, remembering us all in the booth that morning, laughing and joking. I wanted to say it was friendship, but there was something more to it, something physical. I kept remembering the sheen of Avani's hair as it caught the light. Agh, fuck, I was so messed up. I didn't deserve to live.

My mom was home, so Dave parked in the corner of an empty parking lot and lunged for me. Kissing him was completely unpleasurable. If anything, it was confusing and upsetting, as if I was being tested in some way. While beforehand our kissing had been in sync, and we'd known how long to kiss and how to progress through the various stages and types of kissing, here his lips were intruders that my own mouth acted instinctively to fight off. I kept needing to override my own defense procedures and force myself to open up and allow him to continue.

And when we moved to other things, I couldn't have been more bored. I just wanted it to be over, so I went down on him in the back seat, quick and hard, trying to get him off. Afterward I expected him to feel as disgusted as me, but he snuggled close, and I felt the fumes from his face—his breath wasn't particularly bad, it's just that his mouth stank with this human smell, the way mouths do—drifting toward me, and I saw his flabby lips smacking together, asking to be kissed.

He was talking now, but I had fallen into the hole of my own self-hatred. Dave was a good guy, and he liked me so much. Why had I forced him to play this stupid game of mine? He was a human being, not a fashion accessory.

"Relationships are so weird," I said. "It's all about loving another person, but it's also incredibly selfish."

I looked at him as if I expected an enthusiastic response: *Yes, Nandan, I am totally selfish.*

But he shook his head. "Uhh, okay?"

"Well I mean you're supposed to want the best for another person, but you're basically using them."

"I don't . . ." His forehead was creased. "Hmm, I guess what you're saying is that the way we show how much we love a person is by letting ourselves need them."

"Uhh, what? No. You're not getting it."

"So tell me."

"It's stupid. People are supposed to pretend like they're in love, like they really see the other person, but it's all—it's all doomed in the end. And in the meantime it's about—it's about sex—or about looking good at school, or—or—"

I was getting so close to the truth, and I thought at any moment he might leap up and say: *You're breaking up with me.* Instead, he tried to give me a kiss.

"What's wrong?" he said.

"I, ummmm . . ."

Now his eyes got big, and the air was heavy with the smell of his sweat. Raindrops thudded against the windshield, and I couldn't look away from the single stripe of light that fell across his chest.

"I can't do this anymore," I said. "It's kind of stupid, but I don't think I'm actually into guys."

He took a shallow breath.

We both sat up. He rubbed his eyes, then tried to crawl between the seats to get behind the wheel.

"Dude, use the door."

He turned to me, shocked, and I wanted to touch the loose ends of his bow tie, but instead he opened the door and slipped around to the front. I didn't have time to move forward before he started driving, but maybe that was good. I saw him wipe his eyes a few times but didn't spot any actual tears.

By the time we got to my place, he was more composed. "Umm, okay," he said.

I didn't want to get out, afraid he'd drive off, so now it was my turn to slither between the seats.

"We can still be friends, right?" he said.

"Dude, it's not you. I'm just not really into guys."

"It's all right. You don't need to feel bad," he said.

Underneath his words, I could hear him think, *I knew this was coming.* I wanted to speak, wanted to take this all back, wanted not to hurt him, but at the same time I felt a terrible sense of freedom. I never had to see him again if I didn't want to!

My mom wanted to know where I'd been, but when I said, "With Dave," she left me alone, and I stalked past her and shut the door to my room. It was just past one a.m.

223

18

THE LOGICAL PEOPLE TO TEXT about my breakup were Avani and Jess, but I was worried about the consequences it'd have for our homecoming plans, so instead I sleepwalked through that Sunday, watching our group chat like a very pathetic hawk, hoping that Jess and Avani would want to hang out, yet not daring to ask them, and all the time seeing if, in the spacing and frequency of their texts, they might be getting together without me. I told myself they were an old friendship, and I was a new addition, and that if we ever got to be good friends, it'd happen slowly, over the course of weeks and months, but part of me felt small and abandoned.

I was relieved about the breakup, but that sense of wrongness—as if I were living the wrong life—hadn't gone away. Through all this drama, it was hard to escape the logical conclusion: I wasn't the least bit gay; I was a straight guy who'd been living a lie. And so long as I pretended to be queer, I'd never feel right in my skin.

But before I rescinded my coming-out, I needed a final confirmation.

It was Sunday, so not much was going on, but I sent a bunch of text messages, trying to dig up a party that was outside my usual friend group: I didn't want any witnesses to what I was about to do.

A guy from Las Vacas High said, "Totally, my friend's throwing a party," and I got him to pick me up on his way there.

I was afraid the guy knew I was queer now, but we hadn't spoken in almost a year, and maybe this sort of gossip doesn't cross school districts very easily. I asked if there'd be any girls at this party, and he said, "Some." The three guys in the car were pretty run-down, pretty scruffy, and a little on the nerdy side. If it wasn't for me, I wasn't sure any of them would've actually gone out that night.

The party was a small one, just twenty kids gathered in a basement, smoking weed. And because everything was so slow and so anemic, I was a huge hit.

I sat on a narrow couch next to some girls and worked my way into their conversation, cracking jokes, switching my attention from one to the other, and, right when a girl was deciding whether to move closer to me, I popped up, yelling across the room to my friend, and stormed over to make fun of him for something random.

By skipping around the entire room and being friendlier and more high-energy than the other guys, I ended up in a bedroom telling a girl about the problems with my "girlfriend" and how I wasn't sure I wanted to be with "her." The girl massaged my back and my arms and said, "If it isn't right, don't force it," and finally we kissed. She was apologetic that she didn't want to go further, but I was like, "That's fine!" and got her number.

The walk back to Grenadine was incredibly long, and I had to take the back roads, because I was afraid the cops would pick me up for being drunk. I hopped into some bushes when I heard sirens, but I got unbalanced and tumbled down an embankment into a dry drainage ditch.

I had no clue where I was, and somehow I'd lost a shoe, but I still had my phone.

Mari answered after three rings.

"I kissed a girl," I said.

"What's happening?"

"I'm lost, and also I kissed a girl."

"Okay. . . ."

"I'm lying in a ditch, and I kissed a girl."

After five or six repetitions of this, she was like, "Hold on, I'm coming to get you," and I lay there, talking to her on the phone, until a flashlight appeared at the top of the embankment.

When I'd struggled up the side, I said, "Where's your car?"

"I don't have a car."

"Okay . . . where's your Uber?"

"There's no Uber. I walked."

"Oh."

She punched me in the shoulder. "You idiot, what're you doing?"

"I do not feel good."

She plucked twigs and leaves from my shirt, and we sat on a nearby bench, trying to figure out where to go. Eventually she plugged my address into her phone and sighed at me. "All right, come on."

On the way home, I explained everything that'd happened with Dave and with the girl.

"So you don't like guys after all."

"I think so. Possibly."

"But . . . you and Dave hooked up, right?"

"Yeah. Mmm-hmmm."

The conversation was meandering and confusing, but by the time we reached my living room she'd gotten the full picture. As she grew in knowledge, getting steadier and steadier, she even started to tease me for getting so drunk. Meanwhile, I was a little tearful.

"I'm such a radioactive mess," I said.

We were at my living room table. She'd bustled to my room, picking through my clothes, but now her head popped out.

"What? No!" she said. "You're the opposite. You're brave."

"I can definitely see that interpretation."

"It's the only one. You thought you wanted Dave, so you went for it. That's brave."

"No, I, it's—" I gulped, hoping she wouldn't make me go on, but she sat next me, draping one hand over my back.

"What is it?"

"Part of me thinks, I don't know—maybe—perhaps I did this to get close to Avani. Like, like, like, I wanted to be her friend. And this was the only way to get past her guard."

"Ohhh." Mari's lip quivered. "Nobody wouldn't want to be your friend."

She said all the usual things, said I was courageous and caring and funny and fun, but all through her reassurances, I heard the death knell of everything I'd built my life around. I told her that, and she couldn't help but laugh.

"Nandan," she said. "You're being crazy. You had a boyfriend. You'll never not be queer. And if you only date girls from here until you die, then so what? It's fine. It's cool."

"I'll seem confused. Weak."

"It's not weak."

"Look, I know it's not weak. Not really. Not in real life. But people don't want honesty. They don't want mess. They don't want confusion. They don't want awkwardness or second thoughts or . . . or . . . or any of it. They want a simple story. People will laugh at me. I'll be an item of gossip. You know what? I would laugh too. If I heard this story, I'd laugh."

"Well, then maybe you should be a better person." Mari

shrugged. "This really doesn't lower my opinion of you *at all*. Not even a little bit."

"You're not Avani."

"She won't care either."

"You're wrong. She won't be my friend anymore."

"Give her some credit."

"Mmm, we'll see."

Mari's phone rang, and she held up a finger. "One second, it's my mom."

My face froze. It was two a.m. I hung around the edges of the conversation, listening to Mari's side. But it quickly became clear that her mom wasn't mad.

"Yeah, I found him! It's that boy I met on the beach!" Mari said. "Remember him? . . . No. . . . Yes, he was fine! . . . I'm at his place. . . . I think I can stay here tonight. . . . No, I'm okay. . . . No, I don't need to go to the farmers market. . . . Okay, fine, then get me pineapples. . . . Yes, I'm sure . . . pineapples. . . . Okay, I'm good! . . . No, no, don't come over here! I'm good."

When she hung up, I looked at her through one eye.

Mari shrugged. "My mom. She was trying to get me to say our 'I've been kidnapped' word. 'Apricots.' But I used the 'I'm safe' code word instead, so we're good."

"You and your mom are weird," I said. "You told her you were coming to find me?"

"Of course!"

That night, Mari slept on the couch in an old T-shirt of

mine, and in the morning I and my mom drove her back to her place. Her mother met us at the door—a giant woman in an immense caftan—and made us all drink bitter black coffee with her. Mari's dad, a little, sleepy-looking guy—he seemed on the older side—tried to interest us in some YouTube videos, which we watched politely until her mom said, "That's enough, Ben. We have to talk now."

I rubbed my head, which ached terribly, and tried to smile at her. We still had school this morning, and the whole day already felt disheveled and nightmarish.

"So you're Mari's new friend," her mom said.

"Umm, yeah. I think so. Would you describe us that way, Mari?" I said.

"I think we've probably graduated to best friends by now. I'm one of your best friends, I mean," Mari said.

"That seems fair."

"A new best friend!" Her mom swept me into a hug, and my own mother looked delighted too, as if she'd finally found a sister.

The two mothers drove us to school together and then disappeared to have another coffee. Mari was bright and chipper despite her short night, but I was completely wiped out.

"Hey," she said. "I'm gonna go to class. You okay?"

"Yeah."

"Text me if you need anything!"

I sleepwalked through my morning classes. In English I

woke up in a burst of white powder: the teacher had lobbed a chalk eraser at my head.

During lunch, I took a quick circuit to look for Avani and Jess, and I thought of texting to ask where they were, but again I was afraid they'd reject me.

Pothan had stopped texting every day. I didn't get the sense that he was angry, or that we weren't friends anymore; it's just that when you stop responding, people drift away.

I sat with Mari, and she teased me about being mopey.

"You know," I said, "you used to respect me."

She nudged me in the shoulder without apologizing.

In last period, precalc, she started to mock me again, saying, "Hey, Nandan, how'd you sleep last night?" But when she saw my face, she frowned and got concerned.

When we got out of class, I heard a voice call to me from one end of the courtyard.

"Nandan."

Dave, bow tie and all, scurried up to me. "Hey," he said. His damp hair was plastered across the top of his glasses, and his white shirt was spotted from the rain. I looked around, but Mari had disappeared.

"Hey," he said. "You haven't answered my texts. Are you okay?"

Kids streamed around us in all directions, jostling us to keep out of the rain, and we ended up in a little corner between the doors and the lockers.

"I just wanted to make sure things wouldn't be weird," he said.

"Uhh." Things were incredibly weird. Suddenly I thought of Avani, carrying around all that unexplained sadness. I felt diminished, just like her, as if some part of me had disintegrated.

"Because I don't want to stop being friends."

"No, me neither," I said. Right at this moment, I wasn't sure if I ever wanted to speak to him again, but that's not the sort of thing you ever say aloud.

"And we can still go to homecoming together, if you want. I know that's part of your master plan with Avani."

"What?" I said. "What're you talking about?"

"I mean . . ." He looked at the floor, then at me. "You wanted to be her friend. That was . . . being queer . . . this whole thing . . . it's all connected."

"You knew that?"

"Yeaaaaaaah . . . ?" he said. "You've told me that several times, both drunk and sober. Does it really surprise you that I know?"

I tugged on my forehead. "What is happening right now? You *knew*?"

"Yeah . . . you always have a scheme. That's who you are."

"So you guessed I wasn't really—" Just as quickly as it'd filled, the courtyard had emptied, leaving behind only muddy footprints and a few stragglers. "Wasn't really queer?"

"I wouldn't say that," he said. "But did I guess that the

whole queer identification served some grander purpose? Of course. Are you serious? You literally told me this many times. Did you—did you think it was a secret?"

"I mean . . . yeah, I guess. So you're not mad?"

Now his smile got a little pained, and he shrugged. "I'm fine. It's whatever."

"Umm . . ." I bit my lower lip. I was tempted to ask him to come home with me. I suddenly had this weird urge to kiss him. But no, that was fucked! I was the most confused human being on earth! This went beyond bisexuality into seriously sick, twisted, stupid shit.

"Anyway," he said, "I just wanted to talk."

"Umm, yeah."

When we were dating, we never so much as hugged at school, but now he stepped forward and reached around me, our chests touched, and it occurred to me for the first time that he was actually an inch or so taller than me.

That night, after much deliberation, I texted Avani and Jess to say I'd had a lot of fun hanging out with them on Saturday.

Jessie: Same!

Avani: Yep. Homecoming is on its way. I am a diabolical genius—I asked Ken instead of Pothan.

Me: That's actually pretty good!

Avani: I know!

Jessie: Okay, maybe I'm slow, but explain to me why this is good? I thought you didn't even actually like Ken.

Me: It's a divide-and-conquer strategy. Pothan might've said no. Or he could've used it against you somehow. Ken's not swift enough to do that.

Jessie: Or manipulative enough.

Me: Same difference.

Avani: And we've got Niko and Dave all set.

Me: So everything is done.

Afterward there was some small exchanging of GIFs and memes, and I lay in bed, watching the images scroll past, feeling unreasonably gleeful and yet at the same time a bit terrible. I wanted something like a repeat of last weekend, but I couldn't ask for that without seeming sad and desperate.

Dave's words came back to me. He knew it'd all been a scheme. There was something about me that was so petty and so small. The memory of him standing and smiling at me from under his damp hair made me gag from self-hatred.

I typed a message to Jessie and Avani.

Me: Hey, so, Dave and I are still going to homecoming together, but we've broken up.

Jessie: !!!

Jessie: What happened?

Me: I just decided I didn't like him anymore.

Jessie: Are you okay? How did it happen? How did he take it?

Me: He took it okay.

Me: I kind of told him that I wasn't into guys anymore.

Me: Actually I kissed a girl on Sunday.

Jessie: Wow. I mean . . . do you want to talk about it?

Avani: I'm sorry, dude. But it's good you figured it out.

I actually did want to talk about it, and part of me was tempted to text Jessie separately, but the frostiness I got from Avani put me off. They didn't want to hear any of this stuff.

Me: Thanks for getting it. I hope this isn't weird.

Avani: Not weird at all.

Avani: Hope you're okay.

Jessie: Same! See you for homecomiiiiiiiiiiing!!!!! JUST TWO WEEKS AWAY!

19

I ASSUMED THAT NEWS OF my restraightening had gotten around the school, but the gossip didn't get back to me. I spent a lot of time with Mari, and at a certain point I got bored with my own angst. Life became normal. I caught my breath and did my homework and tried to pretend I wasn't a joke.

These past two months were a dream. I couldn't understand why I'd done any of it: made a move on Dave; had a big, flashy coming-out moment; pursued Avani and Jessie as friends; and then broken up with Dave. None of it made any sense to me. I could've just done nothing—kept my job as Pothan's sidekick—and enjoyed being a well-known and well-liked dude.

In public, my skin was tender, as if it were being lightly microwaved all the time. My status in the Ninety-Nine had changed, but I couldn't tell how much was in my head and how much was real. (Maybe it'd all mostly been in my head all along.) Pothan still answered my texts, and I still sat with him at lunch. He never mentioned the breakup. I had to awkwardly slip it into conversation, like I had with Jessie and Avani.

"So, I kissed a girl last weekend."

"Yeah, dude?" Pothan said. "Do you want a medal?"

"If you're handing them out."

I wanted to wipe away the last two months entirely, the whole failed experiment with queerness. And all it took was that one mention about kissing a girl, and the guys were happy to view me as a straight dude again.

But what I'd forgotten about the summer was that I hadn't been happy. So much of the shit we said each day was just nonsense words. *I fucked your mom last night. . . . God, bet you loved being under that man pile in practice. . . . Heard you vomited all over the place at Zafir's party.*

Pothan was clever in how he maneuvered and managed, trying to slot everybody into their place. He didn't allow me to sit there and zone out—he always made sure I came in for my share of the joking. And he wasted no time folding me back into his crew.

"Come on, we gotta get you back out there, dude," he said. "Now you've seen the other side, I bet you're a monster with the girls."

That felt good, but it also established that he was my leader again. Not that I resented him. People like Pothan sought dominance so instinctively that to ask him not to pull these maneuvers, or even to explain to him exactly what he was doing, would've been impossible.

The girls were more awkward about the switch. I tried sitting with Avani and Jess one day, and it wasn't anything you could put into words, I just felt the complete absence of . . . of . . . of any place. I didn't belong at their table anymore. I asked Avani about that guy who'd been liking her photos, and she said, "Oh, that went away."

"Any other prospects?"

"Not really."

"Well you've got Ken to look forward to at homecoming."

She gave me a tight smile. Jess tried to jump in by talking about Niko, but we both withered quickly under Avani's eyes.

Later that night, I got a text from Avani.

Avani: Hey, I need to drop out of the homecoming plan. But you and Jess should have a good time together.

Me: What? Are you serious?

Avani: Lyle's home from Berkeley, and he wants to get together with some people, but if I'm gonna let him use the lake house, I need to be around.

Me: Seriously?

Avani: It'll be fun. You should come, after homecoming, if you want.

Avani: But I know Jess is looking forward to going with you.

I started a dozen angry messages but didn't send any of them. Avani didn't owe me anything, because she and I weren't really friends.

The news hit me harder than my breakup had.

When a friend cancels on you, the reaction ought to be something like *Oh well. That's too bad.* If they're a really good friend, maybe you can say, *Wow, I feel betrayed, but I guess they had a reason.*

What shouldn't happen is that you lie down in bed and find, hours later, that your pillow is still wet from tears.

I couldn't even talk to Dave or Mari about my feelings, because, more than anything, I was ashamed. I couldn't *believe* I had invested so much hope and desire into this person who didn't care about me at all.

During those hours of grief, I didn't even *try* to get over the feelings. Instead, when they began to wane, I did everything I could to whip myself back up into the heights of sadness. I texted Jessie, who sent me back a string of sad emojis.

Jessie: Sorry about this. Avani was really torn.
Jessie: I know she feels terrible!
Me: Whatever.

I had slightly better luck texting Carrie, who, after I explained everything, was happy enough to rage with me for an hour about Avani's shallowness. I was surprised, actually, by how seriously she took the betrayal, and I almost asked her something like *Do you think it's weird I'm so upset about this?*

Finally she had to sleep. I texted Hen, and he was appropriately upset, but he'd never respected Avani, and he made fun of me for trusting her in the first place.

> **Henry**: She only cares about herself.
> **Me**: That's not true.
> **Me**: Okay, well I guess it is.
> **Me**: I don't know! I don't know what it is! I wanted so badly for this to happen.

After texting Hen I realized I was only making things worse. People would hear how upset I was, and they'd think, *Wow, what's wrong with that guy?*

Which was how I finally, after many hours, managed to pull myself together. Hen helped. He texted:

> **Henry**: So are you still going to homecoming?
> **Me**: Err, I don't know. I actually hadn't thought about it. I guess not.
> **Me**: Why? Are you going?
> **Henry**: Err . . . I am making serious efforts to find a date.

Henry: I am out on the internet, beating the bushes, conducting a nationwide search for some hot queer guy who is willing to accompany me.

Henry: And it'd be *really* nice if you and Dave were there too.

Henry: In case you hadn't guessed; I am calling in that favor you owe me.

Me: Umm, yeah, dude, now that you put it that way, of course I'm gonna go.

Henry: Good. This is a promise, right? You're promising me?

Me: It's definitely a promise.

Henry: Now I just have to find a guy.

Me: You need any help with that?

Henry: No. This is something I've got to do.

Henry: As God as my witness, I swear that I'm never going alone to a school dance again.

Me: Well good luck.

So that left me going to the dance, but when I asked around, I found that literally every other member of the Ninety-Nine was going to Lyle's thing. Mari, who I *begged* to come out with us, was shy about coming without a date and said she might just stay home. And even Jessie waffled for a few days and finally canceled, saying Niko preferred to go to the lake house, and anyway she needed to support Avani.

So now I was going to spend this Saturday with my ex-boyfriend at a dance where I'd have no friends.

Dave and I hadn't even spoken since that afternoon when he cornered me and ripped me open, telling me he knew exactly how petty and stupid I was. But I had to text him and tell him that Avani was out.

Dave: So do you still want to go?
Me: Hen really wants us to. Is that okay?
Dave: Of course. We should support him.

20

I WOKE UP ON THE day of homecoming with my arms and legs weighed down by a sense of dread. At ten o'clock, Dave texted me to plan the day. He asked if he could come over beforehand to change, and I said, "Sure," thinking he meant, like, a half hour early. But instead he came a full three hours ahead of time, and we sat across from each other at the kitchen table. Luckily my mom did most of the talking, asking Dave all about his schoolwork and his college visits, and she acted so happy that I couldn't remember if I'd told her yet that we were broken up.

We went into my room to hang up his suit, and he said, "You know, we could still hook up. It doesn't have to mean anything."

After that, I felt an obligation, so I kissed him, and I fumbled at his belt, and my whole body crawled, repulsed by his smell and his touch—I went out of myself, observing the whole thing as if it were a movie—and so I was grateful when my phone lit up with a text message.

"Hen found a date," I said. "Can I see if they want to come over for a while?"

"Sure. Who is it?"

"I don't know. But it's probably really awkward, considering they're just meeting for the first time today."

Hen's response was instant.

Henry: Thank God!

Henry: Yes. Yes. A thousand times yes.

Henry: How soon can we come over?

I showed Dave the text, and he laughed. We were next to each other on the bed.

"Glad we can rescue him," Dave said.

In the silence that came after, Dave inched toward me again, and I said, "You know, I don't think we should do this anymore."

He nodded. "Okay, yeah. Sure. I just . . ." His fist opened and closed.

Looking at my movie posters on the wall, I said, "I can't believe you're not madder at me."

"What? Why would I be mad?" he said.

"Because I'm awful. I broke up with you."

"So?"

"People get mad."

"But you don't like guys. It's no reason to be angry. I mean, well, I don't really *believe* you, but it's still okay." Now his fingertips were a half inch from mine. I moved away slightly, and he took back his arm and rubbed his elbow.

Hen's date was a college guy, a student at Santa Clara University, who had dark hair and a full beard and looked slightly rumpled in his pin-striped suit. He didn't look at all white, and if his name hadn't been Kendall, I would've said he was Indian.

"Yes, like Kendall Jenner," he said.

"Cool."

We sat in my kitchen. Kendall was quiet and self-conscious about his quietness: he kept apologizing for not talking more. This was where Pothan or Avani would've normally stepped up and taken charge, but I wasn't slick enough to do it. My mom could have possibly found something to say, but she'd left an hour ago for a hair appointment. The day outside was cold and rainy. And my apartment was dark and unstylish, with bare white walls and blue carpet. We had no music. Everything was drab and forbidding, and we sat on four folding chairs around the card table where my mom and I ate breakfast most days.

"Err, how did you guys meet?" I asked.

Kendall flashed a quick look at Hen.

"What was that?" I said.

"Huh?" Kendall's dark brow came together.

245

"You guys distinctly looked at each other," I said.

"We met online," Hen said.

"Wait . . . like . . . on Grindr?"

"No!" Hen said. "On Pinterest."

"Excuse me? People don't meet in person off of Pinterest, do they?"

"We are part of a very close-knit subculture," Kendall said.

My eyes went wide, and I felt Dave tense up, as he telepathically told me, *Don't get too excited. They're probably talking about something completely normal.*

"Wha-wha-what subculture? Are you . . . I can't even imagine."

"We like trains, okay?" Henry said. "We're train enthusiasts."

"No. You're kidding. Really?"

All my amusement went completely over Kendall's head. He seemed to have some trouble judging the intonations of my voice, and finally he interrupted, "Are you making fun of us?"

"Well . . . I . . . I don't know."

"I thought these were your friends, Henry," he said.

"Oh my God," I said. "I wasn't making fun. You're train enthusiasts. I'm sorry. That's an unusual hobby. We're not used to thinking of Hen that way."

"It's a passion."

Kendall was completely without humor. Dave took over at this point, and he diverted Kendall onto the topic of trains, where he discoursed volubly. After a few minutes of this, Henry

246

joined in. He wasn't so much into the engineering side of it—he cared a lot more about the urban-planning side. And he had a substantial interest in buses as well.

Dave had no small amount of interest in public transport himself, and he tried to talk about ferries, only to be rebuked by Kendall, who said, "Ferries are inefficient."

"Oh—okay."

"The data are clear on this point."

If there's one thing I knew about the world, it was that I could never have a conversation with someone who said "the data are" instead of "the data is." But Dave didn't have this problem, because now he tried to defend his beloved ferries, and then the conversation got heated and voices were raised, but when Henry got a text message that they had to leave, Kendall seemed genuinely unhappy to go.

"This was excellent." He gave Dave an effusive goodbye. "We should connect online. What is your screen name?" he asked.

"Uhh, for what service?" Dave said.

"For all of them. You don't use the same one for all of them? I'm kenpop."

"Err, I'll find you," Dave said.

Kendall said a brief goodbye to me too, but he did not offer to connect online.

When that experience was over, I slumped on the couch and had a brief moment of terror, thinking Dave was gonna tell me what a great guy Kendall was, but instead he shook his head.

"That was a lot," he said. "But you made them so comfort-able. Avani could never have done that."

I waved a hand at him, but the compliment was welcome, and when he clambered onto the couch next to me, I almost wanted to put an arm around him. Knowing that this would be our very last evening together actually made me miss him, and for a second I thought about unbreaking up. But I told myself no, I'd played around enough with his heart.

When we pulled into Dave's driveway, I said, "This'll be short, right?" I said.

His parents had organized a little party to take pictures and see us off.

"Nope," he said. "It's gonna be so long and so awkward."

"You're really *not* helping."

His house was a cacophony of light and sound. There were old people everywhere, reaching for my hand, and I gave Dave a shell-shocked look, but he was shaking hands too.

His dad clapped me on the shoulder and made me pose for photographs. I stood there, my brain vibrating softly, but they didn't seem to need anything except for me to stand still for numerous pictures.

They told us to eat, and when I said I wasn't hungry they ignored me and put a plate in front of me. I tried to eat some of the cupcakes first, but these were snatched cruelly away, and

I was told to sample all kinds of Chinese snacks that were taken from little foil packages and put on tiny porcelain dishes.

Intermixed with the grandparents and the four uncles and their wives were a bunch of younger kids—Dave's cousins—who looked at us shyly. One girl came up and jabbed me in the stomach and giggled when I made a face at her.

My mom made an entrance a half hour later and was immediately swarmed by Dave's parents, who called us back and made us stand for pictures with what felt like every possible combination of him and me and his relatives and my mom.

Then I was back in the car with Dave, waving goodbye to his family. I felt moderately pepped up. Not completely lost, anyway.

"Hey," I said. "What do you say we just skip homecoming?"

"Nope," Dave said. "We aren't doing that. Besides, you promised Hen."

"But, but, but . . ."

"There are kids in this world who can't afford even one homecoming ticket, and you want us to let two go to waste?"

I snorted. "Okay, but can we leave early if it's awful?"

"Fine," Dave said. "If we mutually agree that it's awful, we can leave early."

"Nuh-uh," I said. "If I think it's awful."

"Yeah, totally, if both of us agree that it's awful."

"No, you're not . . . you're not hearing me right."

249

We went on like this, talking nonsense for the rest of the ride, while I stared at Dave. My brain was doing that crazy thing where it made the curve of his face look so soft and so adorable, and where the sweep of his jacket down the line of his body made me want to, like, throw him onto the nearest soft surface and kiss him. Stupid, hateful, troublemaking brain.

You're bored, I tried to tell myself. *He bores you. Especially the sex. The sex is very tedious.*

Any residual good feelings were blasted away by homecoming. The chaperones knew me, so they pulled me close and tried to sniff my breath, and the vice principal asked where all my friends were. "Ticket sales were low this year," he said. "Is there some other event happening?"

Inside, the music was loud and frantic, and the awkwardness was thick. Without the Ninety-Nine to liven things up, the school was making a poor showing. Almost nobody was dancing. Lots of people were sitting down. Lots of people were looking outward with soft, pathetic eyes. I knew I ought to pull Dave out to dance, but something in my stomach ached, and I just couldn't do it.

We stood in a corner, smiling at each other, and Dave tried to say something, but I couldn't hear him. He repeated it a few times, but I shrugged helplessly. I knew it wasn't nice, but I didn't lean closer, didn't try to make myself understand.

We ended up on a pair of chairs in a dark corner, watching several chaperones sway to the music.

When Henry and Kendall came in, I thought they'd pierce our silence, and Hen did wave and approach, but he was immediately stopped by some girl I didn't know, and he introduced Kendall, who looked very stiff and uncomfortable, but now, in the presence of more and more people, Henry seemed to gleam in the light, and I saw Kendall acquire a look of shy worship.

Henry was much more popular and better known than I could've imagined, and for as long as I looked at him, he was never alone.

Now Dave nudged me and gave me a smile, and I smiled back, feeling my heart sinking. I had a very "on display" feeling. I didn't see anybody looking at us, but in my mind we were spotlighted.

Of course, like always, there were groups of people together, laughing, dancing, having fun, and I *knew* I ought to join them.

I stood up, walked a few steps, but Dave didn't follow, so I sat back down. He rested his head against my shoulder, and normally if we were at school, I'd have pushed him off, but since today was our last day, I put an arm around him, because that's what you do, and we watched all the people moving through the room in their fancy clothes.

Maybe this was a good way of saying goodbye. There really was something sad about it. An entire roomful of kids, and I didn't know their names. I saw them every day, and every one of them was as special and alive as I was, but we passed each other in total anonymity.

I yelled into Dave's ear, "Hey, should we dance?"

"I don't want to. I'm actually enjoying this."

"Really?"

"Yeah! It's nice!"

If it was gonna be our last night, I ought to do what he wanted, so I sat there, wriggling my butt periodically when it was about to fall asleep. All around the room there were camera flashes from what seemed like hundreds of selfies, but Dave didn't make a move to take out his phone and neither did I. Suddenly I had a suspicion that maybe Dave had fallen asleep, but when I looked down, his fingertips were rubbing against the sides of his pants.

The music was quieter now, and we could've talked, if we'd had anything to say.

When a slow song came on, he said, "Do you still want to dance?"

"Well, yeah," I said. "It'd be something to do."

I felt the whistle-hiss of his anxiety as he looked across the crowd.

"Okay," he said. "Let's do it."

On the dance floor, we swayed gently, our bodies close together. Hen, still by the sidelines, gave me a wave, and I felt my insides flare up. I really hated this. Everybody could see us.

But Dave held me close, and his head lay on my shoulder. I saw a chaperone come around, maybe to pull us apart, but after one glance, she smiled and moved on.

"This is nice."

"Yeah."

The music turned quick again, and I transitioned to a faster dance, but Dave stood still, the light shining on his wistful expression. I was about to lead him back to the chairs, but he said, "H-hey, can we leave here without ending the night?"

"Sure. Yeah, of course."

"Because, I—I feel like Cinderella. Like the moment we leave this room, I'll turn into a pumpkin."

"That's not how Cinderella works."

"Yeah."

I took him by the arm and maneuvered him out, rolling my eyes at the chaperones, still standing by the door, ready to smell our breath again. In his car, I heard a sniff.

The moon was bright, and his tears showed up as pale streaks.

"I'm sorry," he said. "I'm sorry. I'm really sorry."

When I touched his shoulders, he uncurled like a starfish and clamped his arms around me.

"This just sucks," he said. "I'm gonna be single again."

"Yeah. That'll be a pain."

He gulped. "Th-thanks for choosing me."

"You were the best homocurious experiment I could've possibly had."

"Not—not Hen?"

"No way," I said. "He and I would *never* have gotten along."

"And it's not—it's not that you just don't like me?"

"Definitely not. If it was any guy, it'd be you." I wasn't certain that was true, but it was the nice thing to say.

Now I took a breath. The collars of our suits rubbed against each other, and for the first time I smelled the cologne he must've dabbed on his neck. My hand reached up, intertwining with his hair.

The look in his eyes was hauntingly tender, and I thought, *This is insane—there's no equality in this.* I don't care about him at all, but he's in love with me. There's no other word for it. What he feels is love. He would do anything, endure any insult, bear any embarrassment, come out to his family, experience the jabs of everybody's eyes—I realized that the coming-out had been even more painful and embarrassing for him than it'd been for me, because Dave didn't *want* attention—and he'd done it just to be with me.

I wondered how I could possibly inspire that sort of agony, when I was just an empty, useless, shallow thing who did nothing more than reflect the brightness of the much more interesting people all around me.

Finally he moved, and our rusty limbs disentangled themselves. I took a deep breath.

"I feel like this dance is winding down."

His eyes drifted toward mine. "It's only nine thirty."

"Yeah, sorry . . . Lyle Brashear killed another homecoming."

"Well . . . I came here for you."

"Thanks, but I don't know. I think the night's done."

"I don't care," he said. "I would've gone to Avani's party. But you asked me to come here."

"Yeah. You're a good friend."

"Seriously. We can go right now to the lake house. I am totally game."

"It's okay," I said. "I'm fine. Can you just drop me home?"

All high school relationships have to end at some point. Everybody knows that. And I was relieved ours was ending so easily. In the car, I smiled and put out a hand, clapping him on the shoulder, and his head swiveled slowly.

"Maybe," he said. "Maybe no more touching."

"What?"

"I think it's good if maybe we don't touch."

I nodded. "Uhh, sure."

He sat silently, and I thought, *Okay this is it, this is the breakdown. This is where everything comes pouring out.*

"What?" I said. "What's wrong?"

When he looked at me, his eyes were wreathed in shadow. The car started, and he turned out into the road.

"Are you okay? What's going on?" I said.

But instead of turning north to go home, he turned south onto Route 17.

21

AS HE DROVE, DAVE'S FACE passed into and out of the shadows. Both hands were on the steering wheel, and his expression didn't shift an inch. Part of me was scared that any minute Dave might explode and tell me that I was shallow and awful and pathetic and confused. And I wanted to say, *It's okay, I know it all, I'm telling myself those things already.*

The crazy thing was that I was happy we were doing this! I'd absolutely hated Lyle Brashear, but he'd always brought a certain excitement to my life, and the combination of him and Avani and Pothan, all together in one house, made my blood flow faster. I couldn't help but think that whatever was happening at the lake house must be insanely epic.

When we got to the house, it was dark and quiet, but lots of cars were parked outside. It was only when the car door opened that I heard the pulse of music. The gravel in the driveway was vibrating from all the bass. And when we turned the knob of the front door, the music blew outward and chewed on the bones in our ears. I reached instinctively for Dave's arm, but then I remembered his voice, *Maybe no more touching*, so instead I beckoned him forward into the dark hole of the living room.

Four or five people danced in front of the TV, and figures shifted on the furniture around us. The kitchen was an island of bright lights, and as we got closer, we heard a yell and the tapping of feet. Pothan slapped a red cup, sending it spraying. Ken, shirtless, let out a whoop that was barely audible above the music. They were playing quarters with a few of last year's Ninety-Nine: kids who'd graduated. Mostly guys, only one girl—a tall nineteen-year-old who kept smiling out of the corner of her mouth but didn't really pay much attention to Pothan's antics.

Dave and I stood next to him. Pothan yelled something, but I shrugged helplessly. With the music so high, he was deprived of his voice. I pulled Dave toward the stairs, where I saw some lights filtering down. Pothan tried to dance, grinding his crotch against my hip while he shouted in my ear, but I ignored him and pushed past.

Upstairs, kids were thicker on the floor. We spotted Gabi, looking a little bored, and I waved hi and asked where Avani was.

"Upstairs."

We kept climbing until we reached the absolute top, the attic, the room where Dave and I had hooked up. Some people, mostly girls, crowded into the stairwell, trying to drink and trying to talk, but we pushed through, into the room, where we spotted Avani—a desperate smile on her face—sitting on the bed next to the large, red-haired figure of Lyle Brashear himself.

He had a knife and a gallon of milk, and he slashed it open, emptying the milk into a garbage can. One of his friends was next to him, shouting something like "This is awesome, dude, this is awesome."

There weren't many people in the room, but he'd taken over its center, where he had tape and plastic and was, apparently, building a bong. Avani was trapped next to him, intensely visible, and now he laid a hand on her knee, while she leaned forward, trying to be interested. I stood in the doorway for a long time, wondering if he'd speak to me. But Lyle was completely in control. At some point, attention shifted, and he screamed, "Kate, what's going on? Come here." His booming voice pulled another girl into the middle of the room, where she drifted, helpless and confused, and fully on display, while everyone else quieted.

Like everyone else, Dave and I were waiting for something to happen. His body was a few inches away, and I almost put my arm around him before stopping myself. The people around us weren't precisely silent, but they weren't joyful either. We were moths, fluttering around Lyle's flame. And yet his light was so weak.

Then out of nowhere, a body crashed into me. "Oh my God!" Mari said. "You're here!"

"Uhh, hey."

Her huge hair pressed into my shirt. "Oh, you look nice too. Wow, I should've gone to homecoming! It's unbelievable how much this sucks."

People couldn't hear us, I was pretty sure, but now that the three of us, Dave and Mari and me, were all turned inward toward each other, we had created a new place for people to stop and come together. Carrie appeared, and she said, "Dude, how was it? Tell me homecoming was terrible. Gabi is so mad I made her come here."

"It wasn't amazing."

"Hey!" Dave said. "I liked it."

The nexus of our conversation grew, and at some point we attracted too much of the room's attention. Avani's head went up, and I saw her wishing desperately to be with us.

"Hey, let's go across the hall," I said.

I opened the doorway across the hall. Two people were making out on the bed, but I turned on the light, and I said, "You guys are taking up way too much space."

The girl popped up, and she grimaced. I didn't recognize either her or the guy, but he yelled, "What the fuck, bro?"

I ignored him, and I kept shepherding people into the room. He tried to get in my face, but I said, "Dude, there's a bedroom open right below us. Go on. Shoo. Shoo." That wasn't true, but I knew if he left he wouldn't come back.

I jumped onto the bed, and Mari clambered on next to me. Carrie sat on one end, and Dave hovered on the other side, his back touching mine.

"Do you guys have a car?" Carrie said. "We drove with Avani. God, I can't believe I fell for that again."

I felt Dave heating up next to me; for some reason he was glowing intensely. I wanted badly to reach for his hand. *Maybe no more touching.*

Gabi appeared in the doorway, and she came in, sitting next to Carrie. Now the bed was full, but the opening of this room had relieved the pressure in the other one, and more and more people came in. Someone threw open the balcony door, and now a few people stood out there too.

Everybody seemed happy. Homecoming was a topic of discussion. People wanted to know about it. Somehow they were very happy that we'd left that place and come to this one: it validated their decision not to go. One really drunk girl said, "Are you back together?"

"No, it's a one-night engagement," I said. But even that didn't make Dave's glow die off.

This room wasn't particularly fun or nice. I hadn't *done* anything. It was just quieter and less crowded. But for now that was enough. And with more space, some of the tension left the crowd. And that wouldn't have been a problem, except that Avani somehow managed to free herself from Lyle's clutches, and she stood in the doorway with a foul expression that put a pall over us all.

Nothing at a T99 party could proceed naturally: If one person was gaining ground, then somebody else was losing it. Avani was free of Lyle, but she also wasn't near the center of attention anymore.

"Sorry I couldn't make it today!" she said. "Did you still have fun anyway?"

"It's okay," I said. "Homecoming wasn't all that great anyway."

"What?" Dave said. "I had fun!"

"Well, I hated not being able to make it."

Her voice drew Lyle, which was a surprise; I'd have expected him to stay in the other room. Now his big body pushed everybody farther into our room. He was in the doorway, projecting his voice all across us all.

"Nandan!" he said. "Heard you'd gone gay."

"Yeah," I said.

"Who's the boyfriend? This kid?" He pushed forward, pinched Dave on the cheek. "Holy shit, is this Bow Tie Dave? You cleaned up all right!"

I hopped off the bed, but Lyle wrapped up Dave into a hug. "Dude, this is awesome. I love this."

Hatred boiled in my gut. Lyle's bushy red hair took up my whole view. He was doing exactly the same shit that Pothan did, but somehow his whole manner and essence were much worse.

"Didn't you two hook up?" he said, pointing to Avani.

"Jesus, you must be gay, to pass up that body." At the silence around him, he held up his hands. "I'm just joking. I'm joking."

I cocked my head, a bit fascinated. Lyle's voice thrashed around, trying to reclaim our attention. I kept expecting him to reintroduce the bong from the other room, but he was smart— he had abandoned that scheme. Now he was operating purely by instinct, trying to hold control simply by talking over everybody. As conversation in this room chilled, he smiled at us. I wanted badly to figure out some technique or trick for shutting him down. Instead, my eyes warred with his, trying to force him to look away, and finally I broke, saying, "Hanging out with high schoolers now?" I said.

"Dude, whoa." He put up his hands. "What's your problem?"

"No problem."

"Come on, man, come on, I always wanted us to be friends. We should be friends. Come on, dude."

He pushed forward, grabbing me around the waist and planting a kiss on my cheek. The movement of his broad body cleared out a swath of space, and everybody pressed together to avoid him. Now with one hand around my neck, he started talking loudly, asking what the fuck had happened, I'd gone gay, Carrie had gone gay, everybody had gone gay.

"Actually," I said, "I'm straight again."

"Ohhh!" he said. "There and back."

The whole situation was uncomfortable, and now, feeling defeated, I tugged at his arm, trying to get out from him, but he grabbed me again, crushing me, before letting me go. I burned with anger, fighting the urge to punch him. Then Dave was next to me, whispering, "Come on, let's go."

Within ten minutes we were out the front door, packed into the car with Mari and Carrie and Gabi. On the way out, I texted Avani to tell her the train was leaving the station, but she wrote back that she was gonna stay.

22

MY FRIENDS BURST INTO LAUGHTER the moment the car started. The laughter continued for some moments without anyone explaining why they were laughing, and I said, "What's so funny?"

"I don't know what they're laughing about," Dave said. "But I was laughing at your face."

Now I burned red as they kept ragging on me. Carrie added, "Oh my God, you really thought you were our savior, didn't you?"

"What do you mean?" Mari said.

"I mean look at him opening that room. He thought he was solving everything. He was so happy. I was like, *This is worth it, just to make him so happy.*"

"Okay, okay, okay. I get it."

We launched into a debrief of the night. In a rare moment

of self-assertion, Gabi took the floor. She was totally confused, and not a little annoyed, over why she'd ended up at this party in the middle of nowhere, instead of going to a perfectly nice homecoming, and Carrie and I tripped over each other trying to explain that Lyle was a legend. A fucking legend.

"That guy?" Gabi said.

For our part, I mentioned how Dave's family had done a total 180 about the gay thing, and I told them about Kendall, which intrigued Mari so much that she made us text Hen to see what he was doing.

"You're such boys! I can't believe you didn't take *any* pictures of him."

"Just picture a werewolf in a pin-striped suit," I said.

"Hey, that's not fair," Dave said. "He was nice and smart, and he really liked Hen."

"A nice werewolf."

We were driving without a destination, until Dave said, "Umm, where should I drop you off?"

Carrie gave an address, and in the passenger seat I struggled to navigate. My blood was up, and I was completely awake. We spent some fifteen minutes discussing Avani. Carrie couldn't understand why she'd thrown this party in the first place.

"It's Lyle," I said. "They have a connection. She's trying to relive last year."

"It was so awkward," Carrie said. "She was totally not herself. She bought all the alcohol, and she got so nervous. And when Lyle rolled in, she was all over him. I was like . . . are you trying to hook up with him? What's going on?"

"No more Avani talk!" Gabi said. "Please!"

This led to Gabi giving all her voluminous complaints about Avani. "She's selfish. And she's needy."

Carrie jumping in to say, "Hey, she's a good friend," and the two of them bickered and bickered, and I had to mediate, saying, "Well, you're both right."

By this point, we were close to Carrie's place, and I had a split second to decide. "We, umm, we could hang out at my place," I said.

There was silence.

"My mom's working, so she won't be around," I said. "Mari and Dave have been there. It's nice. Isn't it nice?"

"Well I can't go home," Gabi said. "I told my parents I was gonna be at my friend Jenny's place."

"That settles it," Carrie said. "Gabi can't go home! We gotta go to Nandan's mysterious lair."

A half hour later, we were in my living room. I fiddled around, arranging chairs, turning down the lights, digging out my stash of alcohol (which nobody drank), while the conversation turned to whether we should order pizza. Gabi was the odd person out, but Mari had cozied up to her, and they talked about some mutual friend who went to Holy Redeemer. My heart throbbed. I didn't have a word for the emotion I was feeling. I looked over my shoulder at the four of them, splayed on the carpet, listening to Mari chatter excitedly. I saw the energy running low, and already a part of me ached with nostalgia for the night that was about to end.

But the doorbell rang, and Hen trotted inside. His voice, clearer and more full throated than anybody else's, rang out sardonically, "Well, I see this is the real party."

Immediately he was peppered with questions about his date, and he, after beating around the bush, said, "I think he has some real potential."

Nobody knew what to say, so I jumped in, "Trains?" I said.

"What? Trains are sexy! And I told you that I was pursuing every possible avenue for finding a date."

"But do you like trains?"

"No, not really. Well, actually, yes. A little bit. I don't *know* what I like. *Surely* you appreciate that, Nandan."

Mari broke into hysterical giggles. She was sleep deprived and jittery, and everything sent her into fits. Gabi was falling asleep in a corner, but Hen added some new energy to the company, and of course all the news of the night—sparse as it was—needed to be related again.

"Oh, I missed Lyle?" Hen said. "I like him—he's handsome."

Another ring of the doorbell brought pizza, and the sprouting of plates and the filling of cups occupied another half hour. I bustled around, smiling megalomaniacally, and Hen said, "Did you two get back together?"

"Nope," I said.

"Well, you're crazy. You look crazy."

My whole face broke into an even wider smile, and Dave sat on the couch, hunched forward, his face intensely happy as he listened to Mari talk with Hen. My eyes took in the fine hairs of his neck, crept across his body, and rested on the broad sweep of his thigh. Dave looked at me, and he slapped the couch next to him. When I got there my knee touched his, but he moved away.

"This is good," he whispered. "I like this."

"Wow, Dave is enjoying a party," I said. "It *must* be great."

Jessie dropped by, bringing the infamous Niko, and a cheer went up from the room—he had formed a not-small portion of the conversation tonight. He went through the room with his sly, laissez-cool attitude. Jessie introduced him to everyone, showing way too much effort, and he refused pizza and soda. He sat in a corner, scratching under his baseball cap, not saying much.

At this point, Hen held forth, describing Lyle's numerous virtues, and Niko, breaking in, said, "Isn't he, like, a total asshole?"

Hen tried to explain: "But he has *style*."

My mood turned. This newcomer was ruining everything. I introduced myself to him, and I saw in Niko's eyes nothing, no recognition.

"Hey," I said. "You're famous."

"Oh yeah?"

"Dave told me about you over the summer. He said you were so hot."

"Really?"

He blinked slowly, and I realized, *Holy shit, I'm doing it. I'm doing the thing I learned from Lyle and Pothan—the thing where I randomly cut other guys down just so I can dominate the room.*

Dave saved the moment by punching me in the side. "He's just jealous," Dave said.

With Niko here, things got a little stilted. Jessie didn't know what to say, so she hung out by his side, trying to tantalize him with some topic or other, even as his silence completely froze up the room.

I solved the problem by throwing Mari at him. She, by now fully amped-up, questioned him about the fanny pack and the baseball cap and the glitter shirt, and he talked at length about fashions in Korea and in the eighties and about some political shit, and it was not uninteresting, but best of all, it freed other people to do what they wanted.

With a nudge, I poked Jessie and asked how her night had gone. By now I could feel the ebb of energy in the room, and I knew the night was fading and dying. Niko's phone buzzed, and he got sucked into a text thread.

The doorbell rang one more time, and Pothan and Ken rushed into the room.

"Wow, shit," Pothan said. "That party sucked. Lyle has really lost it. Carrie, what the fuck, we needed you to save that party."

Pothan pounded a table, demanding some whiskey, and he tried to rope Niko into drinking. Gabi rolled over sleepily, and I told Carrie to put her in my room. I expected them not to come back, but Carrie reappeared, jacket gone, rocking forward onto the balls of her feet, ready to actually get the party started.

And now Pothan went around switching off lights. "It's too bright in here. Shit, it's way too bright." He brought out his phone, turned up the volume, and dropped it into a cup to form a makeshift amplifier. Then he pulled beers out of his backpack: "Picked these up on the way!" He tried to get us organized to play drinking games. Carrie was willing, and they argued over what to play.

Meanwhile I burned with anger.

"It's okay," Dave said. "It's okay. Don't worry. We've had a good time." He hadn't spoken much tonight, but he'd talked enough not to seem out of place.

My whole body was alive to his presence, and I shifted uncomfortably. The rustle of my clothes sent a buzz through my skin.

When even Mari turned her eyes toward the game, I knew I had to act.

"Ken," I said. "Ken, get over here."

His hand paused midway through throwing a ball.

"Hand that off to Henry," I said. "Come on, Ken, we've gotta talk."

With nothing but the power of my voice, I pulled him away

from the kitchen and into the darkness.

Singled out and away from Pothan, Ken looked small and a little confused. "What's going on with you?" I said.

"Uhh."

"Mari," I said. "Didn't you know that girl who liked Ken?"

She gave me a wide-eyed look, then fell into step. "Oh, uhh, yeah."

Ken finally plopped onto a cushion. The game in the kitchen went on for a bit, but Pothan shouted, "What's going on over there?"

When we didn't respond, he drifted over, hanging on to the edge of our conversation. Ken had opened up. "Nah, nah, not Jayne, nah." Mari, now primed, giggled and giggled, and he broke into a big smile.

Pothan hung over us, pausing the game, and he jumped in. "This fucking guy," Pothan said. "He has no game, zero game, Ken can't pull shit."

Suddenly I looked up, locked eyes with Pothan. "Dude," I said.

"What?"

"Dude."

"Come on, it's just the truth."

We looked at each other for a long time, just like Lyle and I had earlier tonight. But this time the energy was completely different. Dave, next to me, radiated good cheer. Ken, sheepish, kept out of the way. All the eyes and hearts were on my side, and Pothan, feeling the unconscious energy of the room, shook his shoulders.

"Yeah, dude, we're gonna get Ken laid," Pothan said. "We're gonna get him laid. It's like I once told you, Nandy-poo, somewhere out there some girl's drawing hearts around your name. And look where that got him!"

Now Dave snorted, and I thought he'd ruin everything by telling Pothan that I'd used his line once, but he stayed quiet.

Pothan lurked around the edge of the conversation, not dominating it, not trying to organize everybody else, but just being cool and helpful, and when Niko got surly again, I gave Pothan a glance, and he ran interference, pulling Niko into his drinking game.

Eventually Niko and Jess left. Carrie had disappeared again. Mari yawned after every sentence, and finally I turned off Pothan's music. Hen surveyed the room. "Well, this has gone dead."

"You want to sleep here?"

"I suppose."

Pothan gave me a high five. "Dude," he said. "We have to hang out more."

"Totally."

"Brunch tomorrow?"

"I like brunch."

Now he leaned close, and he whispered in my ear. "Are you gonna get on that shit?"

Dave was in our hall closet, looking for a pillow and blanket for Mari. I looked at his back. I wanted badly to wrap my arms around his narrow torso, and I tried to remember why exactly I'd been repulsed by him before.

When the door closed on Ken and Pothan, I came up to him. He stared at me, and I stared at him.

"Umm, is my mom's room open?" I said.

"Hen's in there," he said.

"Shit, we need to get him out before she comes home."

"Yeah . . . actually . . ." He was still smiling. "I've gotta get home."

Why would he say that? Why would he ruin this night? But now he went around the darkened room, picking up his stuff, and I was suddenly very aware that we were broken up and that this was our very last night together.

He stood in front of the door, one hand on the knob.

"Thanks," I said. "You've been amazing."

"Yeah?"

"You made this happen. Every bit of it."

"I had fun," he said.

"You weren't bored?"

He shook his head. "No."

"You were quiet. I thought you might be bored."

"I wasn't."

He took a breath. I moved a step closer. *Maybe no more*

touching. I saw a flicker in his eye, and I understood. My face went blank, and I stood there, heart pounding. The doorknob turned again, and I expected to see his smile get wider, but instead I smelled his sweat in the air.

When his hand touched my shoulder, it was clammy. We stood for a long minute. And suddenly that intensity disappeared. I thought again of the pain of trying and trying and it never feeling quite right, and I was about to take a step back.

His bag dropped to the ground. He came upon me all of a sudden, but the kiss was slow and gentle, and before I knew it we'd collapsed onto the love seat.

We had to make out very quietly, for fear of waking people, and we vibrated together in the complete darkness, our hips grinding, my heart rising and falling, our lips brushing against each other endlessly, and when I tried to do more, he said, "No, no."

"Is it because Mari's here?" I whispered.

"No."

"Then what?" A thought suddenly occurred to me: Perhaps this was just our goodbye. Maybe it was this and nothing else.

"It's because sex isn't that great," he said. "And this right now is the best part."

The words took me back to that moment at the picnic table, when I'd thought he was lovesick over Mari, and I'd given him all that heartfelt advice.

His face came down, but his lips didn't touch mine; they only grazed my cheek and forehead.

"Holy shit," I said.

The laugh came from deep in his throat, and he whispered, "Shh," and we kept on touching lips to each other in slow, shimmery time, with our minds fading in and out of sleep, until the first light poked through the blinds.

"Is it morning?" I said.

We were pretzeled on the love seat. Over in the corner Mari was facedown, with an arm flung over her head.

"I need coffee."

"Me too," she called.

Dave mouthed the word "*Yikes.*" I wondered what she'd seen while we thought she was sleeping, and I was embarrassed, though we hadn't done much more than kiss.

"Yeah . . . ," I said. "Let's, umm, let's make some coffee."

Carrie and Gabi emerged. Hen complained about the noise. My mom walked in, eyebrow raised, only to exclaim excitedly when she saw Dave in the living room.

"You're here! You're here! You're all here!"

She was still hyped up from working her night shift, and she insisted on making breakfast. After breakfast, Hen and Mari and Carrie and Gabi all left, and my mom went to bed. Dave and I crawled into my room and collapsed from lack of sleep, only to wake up from a text from Avani.

Avani: Jesus Christ, last night was a shit show. Thanks for coming.

The weekend wasn't over, of course. Pothan and Ken wanted to know what was up. I told them to drop in. Then I texted Hen to see what he was doing, but he had work to do.

Henry: Also, my head feels awful.

I texted Jessie.

Me: What's up with Niko? How did that go?
Jessie: I might be in love.
Me: You want to come over?

She dropped by at the same time as Ken and Pothan, and Dave and I went out with them to a burger place in downtown Grenadine, where we made fun of Jessie for her ridiculous homecoming date while she beamed at everything and everyone. By then, Hen was free, and he dropped by. Pothan and Ken left to use their fake IDs to buy some pot from a store in San Jose, but we saw some T99ers we knew, and they dropped into our booth to talk shit on Avani's party, while we in turn talked shit on homecoming.

Dave yawned. "I have to work on my Mars project."

"Really?"

"Yes."

So I gave him a long hug and walked him to the door of the restaurant. When I came back to the booth. Jessie turned her eyes on me. "So are you two a thing again?"

"Almost definitely? Umm, I think so?"

"You sure?" she said.

"Sure. Of course. . . ." Then I thought for a second. "Wait a second. I have to go! But this was awesome—let's hang out more!"

I ran up behind the unsuspecting Dave and came to a sudden stop next to him. "I'll walk you home," I said.

"You don't have to."

"Sure, but I'm gonna."

I threw an arm around him, crushing him close. My whole brain was filled up with the multitudinous awesomenesses of Dave, and the only possible words to say were "I love you."

He looked at me, and a slow smile crept across his face. "I know."

"Really?" I said. "But . . . I didn't know until now."

"No, it's a—it's a Star Wars thing."

"Oh."

"Trust me, my friends are gonna be *really* happy when I tell them I said that."

"So . . . do you love me too?"

"I do," he said. "I love you so much."

We walked hand in hand, repeating the phrase to each

other, sounding like idiots, and when we stood on the gloomy, rain-choked patio, our kiss was very prolonged.

"I do have to study," he said.

"Let me do it with you."

"No," he said. "No. But let's talk soon."

He waited on the threshold, with all his weight balanced on one foot. I ran a finger up the side of his coat and tugged once on his lapel. "Please?" I said. "I don't know where I'm gonna go. You're just gonna leave me out here, all alone, by myself, to miss you and pine over you and cry about you and be completely pathetic?"

"No. Absolutely . . ." He paused for a second. "No. No."

I looked at him with puppy-dog eyes, and we hovered on the threshold for a solid sixty seconds, with him saying, "No, no, I'm serious, no, I'll get zero work done," until, with a snap of the eyes, I released him from my spell.

"All right, fine," I said. "I'll see you later."

"Totally."

The twin ends of his unknotted bow tie flapped loose around his neck as he took a step inside and, with a fleeting smile, closed the door.

Acknowledgments

Perhaps because this story was so personal, and so deeply rooted in my own shame and confusion and embarrassment over my own sexuality, this novel underwent many revisions and rewrites before coming together. I owe a debt of gratitude to everybody who stuck with this book and who gave me the time and space to finish it.

Peng Shepherd and Amber Burke read a very early version of the book, and they gave me diametrically opposed advice. Peng wanted me to focus more on the dynamics of the Ninety-Nine, while Amber wanted me to drill deeper into the conflicts between the original characters. In the end, I followed Amber's advice more than Peng's, but I'm grateful for both of their feedback. They're talented writers: I read both of their books, then in draft, in the same week back in 2016, and both novels blew me away with their lyricism and insight. They've since given me feedback on several works-in-progress, and I'm fortunate to have found such careful and discerning readers.

My agent, Robert Guinsler, believed in this book from the moment my query hit his email. I knew that if anyone could sell it, he could, and then he did! I've found working with him to be a really congenial and low-key experience. He is exactly what I wanted from an agent, and I'm happy to have found him.

Stephanie Guerdan found my book in the stack of submissions and, with the assistance of Claudia Gabel, convinced Harper to buy it. She's been a wonderful editor, and I really, really owe her for not flinching when the book I turned in after our first round of edits was COMPLETELY DIFFERENT from the one she had bought. I can't emphasize this enough: I don't think I kept even three sentences from the previous version. The changes were for the better, but they did alter some of the tone of the book, and I'm quite pleased she looked at them with an open mind.

Thank you to Renée Cafiero and Erica Ferguson for their copyedits, and to the rest of the team at HarperTeen for helping to put it out.

Erin Summerill and Courtney Sender have been my emotional bulwarks through this whole process. Hardly a day goes by that I'm not texting them. They've seen me through some pretty low times.

The writing community has given me some wonderful friends: Dustin Katz, Jill Diamond, Michelle Kuo, Dominica Phetteplace, and Gordon Jack. And thank you as well to all my friends from the many walks of life: Bradley Heinz, Brian

Pfeiffer, Nahid Samsani. Chris Holt, Claire Rosenbaum, Alisa Whitfield, Sydney Fergason, Will Laves, Donovan Russell, Helen Kwong, and Lisa Gunn. Without you, life would be no fun at all.

I should also thank bupropion and duloxetine. You've been the best antidepressants a writer could ask for. No side effects. No weight gain. And it's a lot easier to write a book when you're capable of feeling feelings.

Thank you to my brother, Sameer Kanakia, and to my parents, Hemant Kanakia and Sonalde Desai. You're a great family, and your love and support are critical to what I do.

My in-laws, Thomas Rutishauser, Karen Sim, and Merilyn Neher, have been unfailingly supportive. Sometimes they get even more excited over my work than I do!

When I was writing the acknowledgments section of my last novel, I was in the midst of falling in love with my now-wife, Rachel Rutishauser. I really wanted to mention her at the time, because I had no doubt that she would be central to my life and to my future, but I thought it would be dishonest, since we hadn't been together when I was writing the book.

Now I face the opposite problem. I cannot begin to describe the love and support she has given me throughout the writing of this novel. She was critical to every part of its composition. My love for her, and hers for me, is woven through each page. So I will limit myself to mentioning one incident.

281

In April of 2016, I went through a bout of depression. I couldn't write. I couldn't do anything. I hated myself and wanted to disappear. One morning I was crying, and apologizing for crying, and apologizing for taking up so much time with my apology, and Rachel said, "No, no, don't apologize. I just wish there was something I could do."

I couldn't make myself feel better, but I wanted to at least make Rachel feel better, so I said, "Bring me . . . paper."

She hopped out of bed and came back with a bound notebook.

"Now bring me . . . a pen."

Two weeks later, I used that pen to write a scene in that notebook, and over the course of three years, that scene grew into this book.